'I still say ... ... ,' said Cassie, as they made their ... ...ugh the warren of cellars.

'Bet you it isn't,' said Matthew.

When they reached it, Matthew prised the door open with his long screwdriver. 'See,' he said. 'Just stuck.'

But Cassie didn't reply. She was too busy staring through the partly-opened door. What stretched ahead for a considerable distance was a tunnel.

'Wow!' cried Becky.

'I wonder if it's safe,' said Poppy.

'The brickwork looks sound,' said Matthew, examining the roof with his torch. 'Come on, let's explore.'

Matthew led the way down the gloomy tunnel, lighting only a small portion of it with his torch. Cassie, just behind him, screwed up her eyes to peer as far as she could.

'Oh look!' called Cassie, craning her neck over Matthew's shoulder.

In the torch beam they could all just make out the shape of a flight of stone steps.

'We've reached the end! Now where will it come out?'

The Ballet School *series*

Trouble at the Ballet School

Mal Lewis Jones

Hodder
Children's
Books

a division of Hodder Headline plc

Children for cover illustration by courtesy of Gaston Payne
School of Theatre, Dance and Drama.

Special thanks to Freed of London Ltd., 94 St Martins Lane,
London WC2N for the loan of dancewear.

First published in Great Britain in 1994
by Hodder Children's Books

A catalogue record for this book is available from the British Library

ISBN 0 340 60732 7

Typeset by Avon Dataset Ltd, Bidford-on-Avon

Printed and bound in Great Britain by
Cox & Wyman Ltd, Reading, Berks.

Hodder Children's Books
A Division of Hodder Headline plc
338 Euston Road
London NW1 3BH

Contents

For Ivan

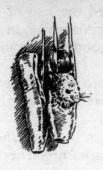

1

A Welcome Back Party

'Oh I can't wait to get back, can you?' Cassie Brown asked her friend. They were sitting in the back seat of her mother's small red Peugeot, heading for Redwood, the famous ballet school.

'It'll be great to see everyone,' agreed Poppy. She was an Australian fellow student of Cassie's who had spent most of the Christmas holidays with the Browns. She had been invited there for Christmas Day and Boxing Day, but after that, Cassie's mum hadn't the heart to send her back to school, knowing she'd certainly be the only girl in the Junior department spending the holiday at Redwood. Before Christmas Day, Cassie had stayed on at the ballet school herself,

1

while she finished the run of Northern Ballet's production of *The Nutcracker*, in which she had had the tremendous good fortune to dance the part of Clara.

As they pulled into the driveway of Redwood Ballet School, Cassie pointed ahead and jumped up and down on the seat.

'That's Becky's car in front!' she yelled.

'Calm down, Cassie,' urged her Mum. 'It's nothing to get excited about.'

Cassie was waving frantically at the car in front.

'Beep your horn, Mum!' she cried.

'No, certainly not.'

At last, Becky turned round and waved back.

'You'd think you hadn't seen Becky for weeks,' said Joy Brown. 'Instead of the day before yesterday.'

Becky had also spent a few days with Cassie, but had gone home in good time to pack.

'I wonder what she's smuggled to school this time?' she whispered to Poppy. Poppy giggled. Last term, it had been a tiny white mouse called Columbus, who had got the girls into a lot of trouble with their fearsome housemother, Mrs Ramsbottom.

It wasn't long before they found out. After Joy Brown and Mr and Mrs Hastings had left, the three girls were alone in Room 12. Becky feverishly began to unzip her case.

'Hope he's all right,' she said.

'Not Columbus again?' asked Cassie. Both she and Poppy were peering over Becky's shoulder. Becky uncovered a small cage and lifted it out.

'No, Hammy this time,' she said, scrutinising him anxiously through the bars. 'I think Columbus has had enough excitement for one year.'

She reached into the cage and took Hammy out. 'He seems OK,' she said, with relief.

'Oh, he's sweet,' said Poppy. 'Can I hold him?'

Becky gave her the small golden hamster and Poppy stroked his short, dense coat. 'Oh look, his front teeth are chattering!' cried Cassie.

'He might be nervous,' said Becky. 'Or hungry. I think I'll put him back in his cage with some nibbles and settle him into the wardrobe. He could do with a sleep after the upset of a car journey.'

'And Emily's Mum will be arriving any minute,' added Poppy.

Emily, like Cassie, had been lucky enough to have a professional engagement with a ballet company the previous term. She, Poppy and Abigail had played the little swans in Birmingham Royal Ballet's *Swan Lake*, together with a Japanese student called Mitsi, who had since returned home. There had been a great mystery when a bouquet of red roses had been sent to Emily at the end of each performance. The last one came with a card, signed by her dad. Emily had become terribly excited by this. Not only was she relieved to hear that her father, who had disappeared months before, was well, but also her hopes were raised that he would make further contact.

Cassie sighed. 'I hope Emily hasn't been disappointed.'

'It must have meant something,' said Poppy. 'Her

3

dad sending her all those roses. I mean, he must still care about her an awful lot.'

'Yes,' said Cassie. 'Perhaps you're right.'

But when Emily walked in with her mother a few minutes later, Cassie could tell by their faces that their Christmas had not been a happy one. Emily looked more miserable than Cassie had ever seen her. And there seemed to be a strained atmosphere between her and her mother. When Mrs Pickering had gone, Cassie tried to find out what had been happening, but Emily closed up immediately. Cassie saw that she'd have to wait until she could get Emily on her own.

Becky tried to cheer Emily up by showing her Hammy in the wardrobe.

'You're lucky Mrs Ramsbottom's not still about,' said Emily.

'Yes,' said Becky. 'It'll be lovely to have Miss Eiseldown back as housemother again.'

'Do you remember how hard it was hiding Tinker from Mrs Ramsbottom?' said Cassie.

Not only had Columbus the mouse shared their room for a few weeks, but, later in the term they had been forced to hide a kitten called Tinker in their room, when Mrs Ramsbottom had asked the caretaker to round up a family of stray cats and have them destroyed. Fortunately, Mrs Allingham, their elderly friend who lived in a cottage in the grounds, had offered Tinker and his brother Marmalade a good home.

'We must go round to Mrs Allingham's tomorrow,' said Becky. 'I've really missed Tinker.'

4

'Let's go at lunch-time if we can,' said Cassie. 'I'm sure Mrs Allingham will be pleased to see us back.'

'I wonder if Tinker will have forgotten me?' Becky mused.

The girls got down to some serious unpacking and soon the room was quite orderly.

'I've had an idea,' said Cassie.

'Oh no,' groaned Becky. 'I know *your* ideas.'

'No, this one's good,' replied Cassie. 'How about arranging a sort of Welcome Back Party for Miss Eiseldown? Just our landing, I mean?'

'Good idea!' said Poppy. 'Let's go and tell everyone.'

'If we put all our biscuits and sweets together, we'd have enough!' said Becky.

'We'd only need yours,' teased Cassie. Becky always brought tons of goodies back to school after each holiday. Becky swiped at her playfully. 'Come on then, Miss Bossy-boots. Let's get started.'

Poppy was sent off to alert all the girls on the landing, while Cassie and Becky set out the snacks they had between them and started colouring a big sheet of paper with felt tips, displaying the message:

WELCOME BACK, MISS EISELDOWN!

Breaking off to have supper, they all scurried back to the landing, hoping to have everything ready before the housemother paid them an evening visit. Girls from other rooms brought contributions of cake, biscuits, crisps and chocolate bars. They decided to cram everyone into Room 12 and wait quietly for the teacher. It was a terrible crush and the girls kept chattering excitedly. Eventually, Cassie had to stand on her bed and shout at them all.

'Come on, you lot. It's not going to be much of a surprise, if she hears loads of voices coming from this room as she walks down the landing.'

The girls quietened down and were soon sitting in silence in the darkness. At last, Miss Eiseldown's high-heeled shoes could be heard tap-tapping down the landing. There were sounds of knocking, doors being opened and closed. Cassie smiled to herself. She imagined Miss Eiseldown's consternation as she discovered the rooms were all empty. The house-mother came to Room 12 last of all and knocked on the door. Cassie had warned the girls not to answer. The knob turned, the door opened and the crush of girls all burst into song:

> *For she's a jolly good fellow,*
> *For she's a jolly good fellow,*
> *For she's a jolly good fe-ellow,*
> *And so say all of us . . .*

Cassie switched on the light. Miss Eiseldown looked quite astounded, but her face was breaking into a smile.

'Whatever have you girls been up to?' she exclaimed.

'We just wanted to give you a surprise party,' said Cassie, grinning.

'Well, you've certainly surprised me! And look at all this food! I'm sure it was meant to last you through till half-term.'

'We don't mind, Miss Eiseldown,' said Becky generously. 'It's more fun eating it all at once.'

Miss Eiseldown laughed. 'Well, let's get stuck in then, shall we?'

She perched on the end of Cassie's bed, munching a handful of peanuts.

'And how did Redwood get on without me last term?' she asked.

'Oh, it was awful!' said Cassie, sitting on the floor at her feet. 'We had a *horrible* housemother called Mrs Ramsbottom.'

'I have heard a little about her already from the rest of the staff,' said Miss Eiseldown. 'I take it she was rather strict.'

'Strict wasn't the word!' cried Cassie. 'Do you know she gave me a black mark one morning just because she found a tiny bit of fluff on my kilt!'

'Well, you might find *I've* toughened up a little,' said Miss Eiseldown. 'My experience of teaching in an American High School was rather alarming after Redwood.'

'Were the kids naughty?' asked Becky.

'Well, more cheeky, really. It was quite a tough, city school. The kids needed firmer handling than ballet students. There again . . .' she looked down at Cassie, 'I'm not so sure!'

Cassie laughed. 'We'll be good, I promise. It's just so lovely to have you back.'

The party spilled out on to the landing as there was so little room, and within an amazingly short space of time, all the food had disappeared.

'And right on top of supper too,' laughed Miss Eiseldown. 'It's a good job you've got plenty of dancing ahead of you. I bet you've all eaten far too much over Christmas!'

Cassie, Becky and Poppy insisted that Miss Eiseldown shouldn't stay behind to clear up.

'Well, if you're sure; that's very sweet of you. I have got rather a lot of things to sort out this evening, ready for lessons tomorrow.'

Noticing that Emily had remained very quiet throughout the party, Cassie asked her to help her carry some rubbish to the bin downstairs. Once they were on their own, she felt able to quiz her once more.

'Did anything happen over the holiday?' she asked. 'You look a bit down.'

'No, that's just it,' said Emily. 'Nothing *did* happen. And I was so expecting Dad to get in touch! How could he send me all those flowers, then just forget about me again?'

'He hasn't forgotten about you, Em,' Cassie said gently.

'Then why doesn't he come back now?' said Emily. 'He's obviously OK.'

'Did your Mum expect him to return?' asked Cassie.

'No. She said I was silly to expect anything from him. And she's been really upset over Christmas. Oh, Cassie, it's just made things ten times worse!'

Emily promptly burst into tears and Cassie hugged her until she'd finished crying.

'I think Mum blames me for reminding her again,' she sobbed.

'Well, you didn't ask your dad to send you the flowers,' said Cassie. 'It's not your fault. Believe me, Em.'

Emily wiped her eyes with her sleeve. 'It was a rotten Christmas,' she sniffed.

'Well, put it behind you, now,' said Cassie. 'Look forward to the term ahead and just forget about home as much as you can.'

'But it's hard not to think about it all the time.'

'Think about your dancing instead,' Cassie suggested. 'You got Honours for your Pre-Elementary last term. You're doing really well.'

Emily made a visible effort to look more cheerful. 'You're right,' she said.

'I'm always right!' Cassie joked.

As they walked away from the bins, arm-in-arm, they bumped into Matthew. He wasn't looking too happy either.

'Have a good Christmas?' Cassie asked him.

'Terrible,' groaned Matthew.

Emily looked quickly at Cassie. 'You stay and talk to Matthew,' she said. 'I want to get back to the room!'

Matthew looked at Emily's receding figure.

'Has Emily been crying?' he asked.

'Yes,' said Cassie. 'She's got problems at home.'

'Oh sorry,' said Matthew. 'I didn't mean to butt in. I had a pretty useless Christmas too!'

'Why?'

'My academic grades have slipped a bit and my parents reckon I'm wasting my time here. They forget about all the dancing we have to do!'

9

'Well, you'll just have to be patient with them,' said Cassie.

Matthew grinned wryly. 'Have you ever known me be patient?'

'Well, no,' said Cassie with a smile. 'But you could try it some time!'

'Oh well,' said Matthew. 'It's a relief to be back at school anyway. See you tomorrow. It's maths first, isn't it?'

'Right,' said Cassie. 'And no Mrs Ramsbottom!'

'Great, I'd forgotten!' said Matthew. 'Well, that's something to feel cheerful about at least.'

Cassie took her leave of Matthew and returned to Room 12 to help finish the clearing-up. When she climbed into bed at half past eight, her mind returned to the conversations she'd had with Emily and Matthew.

I'm beginning to feel like an agony aunt, she thought to herself and fell asleep wondering how to lift Emily's spirits.

2

The Unders And Overs

Everyone felt stiff and out of condition in ballet class the next morning. Christmas was not a good time for keeping up dance practice. But Miss Oakland, their ballet mistress, didn't make any allowances for this fact, nor for the quantities of mince pies, plum puddings, sweets and Christmas cake which had been consumed during the previous few weeks.

Cassie was jolly glad she had been dancing in *The Nutcracker* right up to Christmas Eve, otherwise she would have felt even more out of practice than she did now.

Miss Oakland looked as trim and streamlined as ever. She wore a smooth, black dress, flared from just below the waist and her hair was pinned back in a large bun. She was attractive in a severe kind of way, but her face never betrayed any warmth.

She nagged and carped all through the lesson. When they did their pirouettes she said they were about as graceful as penguins on ice, and she likened their pas de chats to soggy trifles.

The girls gritted their teeth and tried harder. How Cassie hated these first few ballet classes after a holiday. The ache in her leg muscles started to become unbearable. She daren't stop in the middle of the exercise, but after finishing her assemblés, she stooped to rub her aching calves.

'What's the matter, Cassandra?' Miss Oakland immediately snapped. 'Dancers don't give in at the first twinge!'

'My legs are aching, Miss Oakland.'

'Of *course* they're aching. I wouldn't be doing my job properly if they weren't.'

She walked across to where Cassie was standing in the second row.

'May I just remind you, Cassandra, while we're on the subject of working hard, that your exam result last term was very disappointing. Not unexpected however. I told you all along that you weren't working hard enough.'

Cassie looked at her feet. She didn't need reminding that she had only received a Pass for her Pre-Elementary exam.

'Others in the class,' went on Miss Oakland, 'worked consistently and reaped the benefits. Abigail, Emily and Poppy are to be congratulated on gaining Honours.'

With the excitement of Christmas and *The Nutcracker*, Cassie had pushed her disappointment to the back of her mind. Now it re-surfaced sharply. She could tell Miss Oakland hadn't forgiven her yet for slacking.

At the end of the class, Miss Oakland spoke to them about the Junior Shield, which was awarded annually at the end of the second year.

'The shield is given to the most outstanding girl ballet student in the second year,' explained Miss Oakland. 'And there is an equivalent cup for the boys.'

It was a reminder that after this year, those students who were lucky enough to be invited back, would be joining the Senior section of the school. But Cassie's mind was filled with gloom. She had had such a poor exam result; her chances now of being awarded the Junior Shield were very slim indeed. *Perhaps Emily could win it*, she thought, with an impulse of generosity. *That would make amends*.

But then she thought to herself that perhaps all was not lost, and resolved to work very hard for the next two terms.

In the changing-room afterwards, Abigail came over to their little group.

'It was nice of Miss Oakland to congratulate us, wasn't it?'

'Yes,' said Poppy. 'But we deserved it.'

Cassie bit her lip. Abigail and Poppy could be tactless at times.

'Are you speaking to Celia yet?' asked Poppy.

'Well, yes,' said Abigail. 'It seemed a bit mean to carry on ignoring her.'

'Sh, she's coming over,' said Emily.

Celia was in her 'sweetness and light' mode, which Cassie and the others found even more irksome than her rudeness. They all found it very hard to forgive her for being such a sneak when Mrs Ramsbottom had been in charge of their landing.

It soon became obvious that she was trying to ingratiate herself into their gang, especially as she'd noticed that Abigail was more friendly with them now.

'Did Father Christmas bring you all the pressies you wished for?' she asked.

Cassie was the only one who could be bothered to answer. 'Oh, yes thanks, Celia. How about you?'

'Well, more or less,' Celia replied. 'I had a new computer, but I was a bit disappointed they only got me two games to play on it. I soon got fed up with them.'

Cassie made an extra effort to get dressed quickly, so that she could escape with Becky without Celia tagging along.

Their first academic lesson of the term was maths. What joy it was to see Miss Eiseldown sitting at the teacher's desk when they entered the room. Cassie shuddered as memories of Mrs Ramsbottom sitting there came back.

Miss Eiseldown started them off on quite an interesting assignment. It was to make a box, of any shape, out of card, using accurate measurements.

14

After some thought, Becky chose a chocolate box, and Cassie a box in the shape of an upright piano. Miss Eiseldown said this was the most original idea in the class, and hoped Cassie would be able to make it precisely enough for it to look right. Design and preparation took the whole of the double period and the girls and boys were asked to finish making their boxes for homework.

'Wow, that was so much more interesting than the stuff we were doing with Mrs Ramsbottom,' said Cassie, as they filed out into the corridor.

The next lesson was music; Cassie and Becky were surprised when Mr Green called them over to his desk.

'I think you two are about ready to join the school orchestra. You're both studying for Grade Four, aren't you?'

The girls nodded.

'Well, first practice is at lunch-time today. Can you make it?'

The friends said they could. After lunch, they set off to the hall with their instruments, feeling both nervous and excited.

'I'm not much good at sight-reading,' Cassie confessed to Becky.

'Just listen to everyone else. You'll soon pick it up, with your good ear for music.'

Becky was a quick sight-reader and had no problems at all during the practice. Cassie, on the other hand, struggled to make sense of the black tadpoles on the page on the music stand before her. *If only they would keep still and stop wriggling about*, she thought.

But the more she stared, the more they squirmed. Remembering Becky's advice, she pretended to play until she'd heard the passage a few times and was able to reproduce it from memory.

At the end, Becky moved across to Cassie from the cello section and asked if she'd enjoyed it.

'I think so,' said Cassie. 'I guess it'll get easier. Especially when I've practised the piece on my own.'

'Oh, watch out. Here comes Celia!'

'Hello, you guys,' said Celia, rushing up to them. 'Welcome to the orchestra. It's fun, isn't it?'

'Yes and no,' Cassie answered.

'Of course, when you're an old hand like me,' said Celia, 'you know what's what.'

'Well, er, we were just going, weren't we, Becky?' said Cassie.

'Yes, must dash,' agreed Becky.

'Oh, I'll tag along with you. Got to go back to the landing, haven't we? To take our instruments back?'

Cassie and Becky looked at each other in dismay. But there was nothing for it. They had to listen to Celia lecturing them about the school orchestra all the way back to the girls' wing.

'Honestly,' said Cassie later. 'She can't take a hint, that girl. You have to be rude to get rid of her!'

'Thank goodness she didn't insist on coming into our room,' said Becky. 'Poppy had got Hammy out for some exercise.'

'Let's get him out again now, shall we?' said Poppy. 'I do love playing with him.'

So Hammy was brought out of the wardrobe again

and allowed the run of the room, while the girls settled down to the task of making their boxes for maths.

'There, that's finished!' Cassie announced some time later. She held up her miniature piano proudly.

'Wow, Cassie, that looks really professional!' said Becky, who was just putting the finishing touches to her chocolate box.

'Help!' cried Poppy suddenly. 'I can't get the sides of my pyramid equal.'

'Let me have a look,' said Cassie, putting her own box on the floor, and going to Poppy's aid.

Emily had problems with her box, too, and by the time Cassie and Becky had helped Poppy and Emily finish off, it was bedtime.

'Where's Hammy?' Becky cried suddenly. They had all forgotten about him; they had been concentrating so hard on their homework.

A frantic search was soon under way, but Hammy could not be found.

'Miss Eiseldown will be here in a minute to check our light's out,' said Becky, anxiously. 'We must find him.'

'He may have hidden in a little nook somewhere,' said Cassie. 'Don't worry, Becky. He'll probably stay quite still when Miss Eiseldown opens the door. We'll just have to look for him when she's gone back upstairs.'

The girls quickly got into their pyjamas, jumped into bed and switched off the light. Just in time.

Miss Eiseldown put her head round the door and wished them goodnight.

'Goodnight, Miss Eiseldown,' they chorused.

They could hear her doing the same all along the landing. At last came the sound of her high heels clattering up the stairs.

'There, safe now,' said Cassie, snapping on the light.

Poppy, Cassie and Becky got out of bed again, but Emily said she was too tired to hunt for the hamster any longer.

'Oh look,' said Cassie, 'I've left my piano box on the floor. I'd better pick it up in case it gets trodden on.'

As she lifted it up, Hammy fell out on to the floor.

'Oh, there you are!' exclaimed Becky, pouncing on him.

He had chewed the bottom and back of the piano while he had been sheltering in it. Cassie gazed at it with a stricken expression.

'My beautiful piano!' she cried.

'I'm so sorry, Cassie,' said Becky. 'But you know what hamsters are like.'

'Well, I do now,' said Cassie. 'I can't give my box in like this. What shall I do?'

'You'll have to ask for more time,' said Poppy. 'Bad luck, Cassie.'

Cassie went to bed in a bad mood, but woke up next morning inexplicably full of the joys of spring.

'I'll help you do your box at lunch-time,' Becky offered. She had begun to feel rather guilty about Hammy's misdeed.

'No, I'll do it this evening. It's a nice bright day. Let's have a walk over to Mrs Allingham's.'

Becky smiled warmly. 'Oh yes, that would be lovely.

18

I can give my Tinker a cuddle. Are you going to come, Emily?'

'No, I don't think so, thanks,' said Emily. 'I want to practise some of the new ballet enchaînements.'

'What about you, Poppy?'

'I'd love to,' said Poppy.

And so three of the four made their way across the lawns, past the folly, and to the edge of the wood, where Mrs Allingham's cottage lay.

After they'd thawed out by Mrs Allingham's log fire, sipping cups of hot cocoa, Cassie asked her if she'd had a good Christmas.

'Oh lovely, thank you,' she said, her eyes bright. 'My daughter and grandchildren came over from Norfolk. I don't see them often.'

'Is she a dancer?' asked Poppy.

'No, not any more. But she did dance in a few West End musicals before she had her children. There they are, look – in those photos on my mantelpiece.

'That's Emma, my daughter. And these are my grandchildren – Robbie and Rachel.'

'Oh, they look sweet,' said Cassie. 'So where did Emma train?'

'At Redwood of course!' exclaimed Mrs Allingham with a smile. 'I taught her myself.'

'That must be unusual,' said Cassie. 'For a mother and daughter to be at the same ballet school.'

'Well, of course, I was at the ballet school myself as a child.'

'I didn't know that!' cried Cassie. 'You're a dark horse, Mrs Allingham!'

19

Mrs Allingham chuckled. 'Well, I have to keep a few secrets to myself.' Her eyes went misty. 'I'd give a lot to have those days all over again. To be young and learning to dance. And see all my old friends. We did have some fun together.'

'Tell us about it,' pleaded Becky. 'You always have such lovely stories about things that have happened.'

Mrs Allingham reflected for a moment. 'Well, one of the most exciting things we used to do was The Unders and Overs.'

'The Unders and Overs,' repeated Poppy.

'Yes. It was a race which took you under the school and over the school – the main building, of course.'

'I don't understand,' said Cassie.

'I get it,' said Becky quickly. 'Under would be the cellars, and over would be the attics.'

'Quite right, Rebecca,' said Mrs Allingham. 'We used to do it just before Christmas, when it went dark really early. It was quite spooky in those cellars in the dark.'

'I suppose if there was a crowd, it wouldn't be too frightening,' said Cassie.

'Oh no, we didn't do it together. It was a timed race. Each of us went alone.'

'Oh, that does sound spooky,' said Poppy. 'Were you allowed a torch?'

'Oh yes. A torch was essential. There is no proper floor in the attic. You have to pick your way across the rafters.'

The girls sat spellbound while Mrs Allingham told them all about the races she had taken part in.

'Isn't it an ace idea?' said Cassie, on their way back to school. She did a little jig on the spot.

'I'm not sure,' said Becky. 'Sounds a bit scary to me.'

'Oh come on, Becky,' said Cassie. 'Let's tell Emily and Abi and Matthew about it. We could organise a proper race.'

'I've got a stop-watch we could use,' said Poppy excitedly. 'And a torch.'

'All right,' Becky agreed. 'Anything for a laugh.'

'The Unders and Overs,' announced Cassie grandly, 'is to be re-launched at Redwood!'

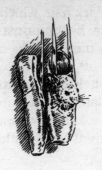

3

Who Will Be Cinderella?

The Unders and Overs race wasn't far from Cassie's thoughts the next day. But before she had a chance to speak to Abigail and Matthew, there was excitement of a different kind.

Tap dancing was a surprise new lesson on the timetable this term, and the girls went off to their first tap class full of enthusiasm. Cassie didn't know quite what to expect as she hadn't ever taken tap lessons before.

Their second surprise was that their new teacher was a man – Mr Whistler. He looked very young; Cassie guessed he had probably only just finished his training. Mr Whistler was also very good-looking, with an abundance of black hair, which he wore parted in the middle. When he demonstrated a short tap sequence to them, the long bits of hair at the front kept bobbing over his eyes.

Cassie couldn't help smiling to herself – but she recognised he was an ace tap dancer. Both girls and boys in the studio looked very impressed and listened and watched intently as Mr Whistler showed them the first step.

He explained he was starting with the basics, as not everyone had had previous training. Cassie smiled her thanks – but despite what he'd said, as the lesson wore on, the young teacher seemed to be teaching them one new sequence after another.

'Phew, that was a bit of a struggle,' Cassie complained afterwards. 'It felt like a crash course!'

'Yes,' agreed Poppy. 'He did seem to be cramming an awful lot into an hour.'

'Well, I thought it was wonderful!' cried Becky. 'The best dancing lesson I've ever had.'

'It's all right for you,' said Cassie. 'You've done tap before. Have you, Emily?'

'I have done a little, but it was years ago,' she answered.

'If we're quick,' said Cassie, 'we could catch Matthew before the next lesson and tell him about the Unders and Overs.'

'I thought it was amazing you hadn't mentioned it all morning!' said Poppy.

'What are you talking about?' Emily asked.

'Oh, I forgot to tell you,' said Cassie, reddening

24

slightly. 'I don't seem to see much of you these days! It's a race. Come with us now and you can hear all about it.'

'Shall I go and grab Abigail?' suggested Poppy.

'Good idea,' said Cassie. 'But make sure Celia doesn't follow you.'

Matthew and Abigail were very excited about the race and were all for holding it that very night.

'No,' said Cassie. 'I've been thinking about when we should do it, and I think I've hit on the perfect time.'

'When?' asked Becky.

'Well, you know Miss Eiseldown told us there's going to be a full staff meeting a week on Thursday? That would be the perfect evening!'

The others agreed wholeheartedly and a time was fixed for the race that Thursday night.

'Oh, isn't it exciting?' Cassie whispered to Emily, as they walked along the corridor to their next lesson.

'Yes, I suppose so,' said Emily, shrugging.

'You still don't seem very happy, Em,' Cassie remarked.

'Oh, I'm all right. Don't worry about me.'

But Emily didn't seem to join in much with her room-mates any more. In fact, she seemed to spend most of her spare time in the practice rooms.

'Look, aren't you working a bit too hard?' Cassie said.

'I want to succeed,' said Emily. 'That's the most important thing to me now.'

Her mouth looked very set, and Cassie could guess

25

how she was pushing down all thoughts and anxieties about her family.

'Fair enough,' said Cassie. 'But don't forget your friends. Are you going to take part in this race?'

'I don't think so,' said Emily.

'There you are! You never join in any more. Oh, go on Em. I want you to take part. It's going to be amazing.'

'Oh, all right,' said Emily reluctantly. 'If it will stop you going on at me!'

Cassie was about to answer when everything went dark. Someone had put their hands over her eyes.

'Guess who?' said a funny, croaky voice from behind her.

'I don't know,' said Cassie. 'Give me a clue!'

'Best-looking boy in the Juniors,' croaked the voice.

'Matthew!' guessed Cassie, quite correctly. 'You nearly made me jump out of my skin.'

Matthew laughed and then caught sight of Emily's face.

'Sorry,' he said. 'Have I barged in on something?'

'No, it's all right,' said Cassie. 'We'd finished.'

'I was thinking,' said Matthew.

'Did it hurt?' Cassie quipped.

'About the Unders and Overs!' Matthew went on.

Cassie immediately started to pay attention.

'We need to know the lay-out of the attics and cellars.'

'I wonder if I should ask Mrs Allingham?' said Cassie. 'On the other hand, she might not want us to do the race.'

'That's right,' said Matthew. 'Grown-ups are always describing the wonderful things they used to do in their childhood. But if you try to copy, they soon say no.'

'I'll think about it,' said Cassie. 'And if I have any ideas, I'll let you know.'

The next morning, Cassie woke up feeling rather breathless. *Perhaps I dreamed I was running the race*, she thought. As soon as she'd sat up and drunk the glass of water which stood on her locker, her breathing became more relaxed. She thought no more about it as she became involved with the events of the day.

Miss Oakland had some news for them in ballet class which, for a while at least, put the Unders and Overs race in the shade. She told them the second years were going to be given the opportunity to make a concert tour of Northern France, in the forthcoming Easter holiday.

Cassie nudged Becky, who was sitting cross-legged beside her, and grinned.

'Miss Wrench is writing to your parents today, for their consent,' said Miss Oakland. 'Of course, you will all be expected to participate.'

'I wonder if it'll cost much?' whispered Cassie to Emily, who was on her other side. Emily was evidently wondering the same thing and looked quite glum.

'Excuse me, Cassandra,' called Miss Oakland. 'Did you want to say something?'

'Oh – no thank you, Miss Oakland,' stammered Cassie, flushing.

'Well, if I can continue without interruptions,' the

ballet mistress went on. 'The tour will last seven days and in that time we shall be giving four performances. I expect you are wondering what we shall be dancing for our French audiences?'

A murmur ran round the class; an invisible question mark hung over each student's head.

'Well, Madame and I have chosen Cinderella. As you probably know, it's a French fairy story, so it seemed ideal. We'll be using the Prokofiev music for the ballet. I think you'll all like it.'

Cassie had only seen the ballet once, and that was on television one Christmas. After class, she chattered with her friends excitedly.

'I wonder who'll be Cinderella?' said Abigail, not able to disguise her own hopes.

Cassie found the question difficult to deal with. Fortunately, Becky, who never had any dancing ambitions, answered before she had to.

'The student who does her audition best, of course!'

'Miss Oakland said Madame would tell us about parts to learn and when the audition was,' said Poppy. 'So there's no point worrying about it until she tells us more.'

Emily was studying herself in the changing-room mirror.

'I'd love to be Cinderella,' she said and then sighed. 'But Cinderellas are usually thin and beautiful!'

'Well, you're not exactly fat and ugly,' said Cassie, laughing. 'That's a point – who'll be the Ugly Sisters, I wonder?'

'Now, that's more my style,' Becky broke in. 'Yes, that would be a lot of fun.'

When Madame Larette gave them further details later in the week, Cassie, Poppy, Abigail, Emily and Celia all chose to audition for the main parts of Cinderella and the Fairy Godmother.

Becky stuck to her guns about wanting to try for the part of one of the Ugly Sisters. She would be competing against Matthew and three other boys, but no other girls. This didn't seem to bother Becky in the slightest.

Cassie couldn't help admiring her; she half-wished she wasn't bothered about the leading role herself, as it was uncomfortable being in competition with some of her best friends. But you had to get used to that in dancing; you had to accept that sometimes you would be lucky, and sometimes you wouldn't.

Secretly, though, Cassie felt sure she would have a very good chance of being chosen as Cinderella, because of her experience of dancing Clara professionally at Christmas.

That evening the girls were excited and rather restless. They let Hammy out for his usual evening romp and it was as though he was infected with their high spirits. He raced around like a crazy clockwork mouse, and when Becky tried to catch him to put him back in his cage, he refused to keep still.

The room soon became chaotic – with all the girls chasing the little hamster. In the end, Becky had to stop them all.

'Let's just sit quietly a while,' she pleaded. 'He's

29

getting sillier and sillier. And all this noise and laughter isn't helping much.'

Cassie, who had been the worst culprit, lay on the floor until her giggles had subsided.

'Ooh,' she said, clutching at her sides. 'It hurts from all the laughing.'

As the room quietened, Cassie was conscious suddenly of her breathing. She was out of puff from chasing Hammy, but there was something else. A kind of choking feeling which stopped her from breathing properly. Her head began to feel very hot and she lurched across to the sink for a drink of water.

'Can't you keep still, Cassie?' Becky chided. 'I've just got Hammy cornered.'

'I can't breathe!' gasped Cassie.

'You shouldn't giggle so much!' Becky called.

Cassie hadn't the breath to say any more, but just stood, clutching the sink, while Becky advanced on her hamster.

'Oh no!' Becky cried. 'Hammy's wedged himself in my ballet shoe now!'

'Can't you pull him out?' asked Poppy.

'No, he's too fat. He's got himself stuck.'

'Oh what can we do?' cried Poppy.

'I'll have to cut the shoe,' said Becky.

'You can't do that to a good ballet shoe!' cried Emily.

Becky was looking uncertain. 'I'm not sure I can anyway, without injuring him.'

'Try squeezing him out, like toothpaste,' suggested Poppy. 'Here, let me help.'

The two girls squeezed gently on the pink satin and – POP – out plopped the fat yellow hamster, his whiskers twitching. Becky just managed to save him from falling on his head.

As Becky and Poppy fussed over Hammy, once more safely in his cage, Emily moved over to Cassie.

'Are you all right?' she asked

'Yes, I'm OK now, thanks,' said Cassie. 'Just had a bit of a funny turn.'

'Come and sit down on my bed,' said Emily. 'You don't look too good.'

Cassie actually felt much better, but followed Emily anyway. 'Have you heard anything from your mum yet about the tour?' she asked.

Emily sighed heavily. 'Yes, I had a letter this morning. She really can't afford to send me. It's over a hundred pounds!'

'What about the bursary?' asked Cassie.

'I've still got to budget for two terms' equipment, so I'm not really sure.'

'Well, until you are, you must give yourself the chance to audition. You mustn't give up yet.'

'I won't,' said Emily. 'But, Cassie, wouldn't it be awful if I were chosen to be Cinderella, and then I couldn't afford to go on tour?'

Cassie felt helpless in the face of her friend's problem and was quick to change the subject.

'Will you come to the library tomorrow with me? I want to see if they've got any books on Redwood that might tell us something about the cellars and attics of the old house.'

31

'I'd forgotten all about the Unders and Overs,' said Emily.

'I hadn't!' said Cassie, smiling.

4

Trouble In The Attic

In the school library the next day, Cassie found two
volumes which included photographs of Redwood, as
it had looked many years ago. She showed Emily one.

'Look, it's quite different with all that ivy growing
over it, and no boys' wing or studio block.'

As Emily pored over the photos in one book, Cassie
looked up references to Redwood in the other.

'Here we are!' she said excitedly. 'There's a plan in
the appendix. And it includes the cellars and attics.'

'We should photocopy it,' said Emily, catching some
of Cassie's enthusiasm.

The librarian asked what it was for.

'A History project!' Cassie quickly explained.

'A funny History project!' said Emily, later.

'It's what's called the hands-on approach,' said Cassie. 'It wasn't really a lie, was it? The Unders and Overs is an historical ritual, which we are planning to revive.'

Emily looked unconvinced, but Cassie didn't let that dampen her enthusiasm. After Emily had left her to go to a practice room, Cassie sought out her other friends, to show them the plan.

'That's just what we need!' cried Becky.

'Well done, Cassie,' said Poppy.

'Let me have a look,' said Matthew, who was craning over the girls' heads. 'We should be able to plan a route now.'

'Yes,' said Cassie. 'We'll work it out tonight, and then next week we can all mark it out together before the race itself.'

'You mean, actually in the attics and cellars?' asked Poppy.

'Yes,' said Cassie. 'So we know exactly where we're going.'

'That's a relief,' said Poppy. 'I thought we were going to have to follow the plan. I'm hopeless with maps and things.'

'Typical!' said Matthew.

He was quickly shouted down, but Cassie noticed his face looked anxious, rather than high-spirited. She led him over to another area of the yard, once the meeting was over, to ask him what was wrong.

'Oh just parent trouble,' said Matthew, in answer to her probing.

34

'But you haven't been home for ages!' said Cassie in surprise.

'I know, but they can still write to me, can't they?' Matthew retorted.

'What did they say?'

'Basically that I need the time to catch up with my academic studies. They're not willing to pay the fees for the tour, because I haven't been working hard enough.'

'Oh, poor Matthew, you were so looking forward to being an Ugly Sister!'

'I shall still audition,' he said firmly. 'If I can't get round my mother, I shall ask my grandparents. I'll get to France somehow, you'll see!'

'Good for you!' said Cassie.

The next week passed in a flurry of learning short extracts for the Cinderella audition and planning the Unders and Overs. As luck would have it, the audition was going to fall the day after the race. Cassie didn't know which event was causing her the greatest excitement.

She had given the others strict instructions to gather in her room immediately after supper on Thursday. This they did, all wearing lightweight pumps which would not clatter along the attic floor. Poppy had her torch and stop-watch ready.

'Now, you've all seen the plan, and the route we've marked,' Cassie announced. 'All we need to do now is to walk over the route together, before we start the race.'

'Will we have time to do all this before the staff meeting's finished?' asked Emily.

'Of course we will!' said Cassie airily. 'You know how long the Wrench's meetings last!'

'I think I'll bring my torch,' said Emily. 'One won't be enough between six.'

Cassie took Poppy's torch and led the way to the back of the wing where a little flight of steps led down to the cellar door.

'What if it's locked?' asked Becky.

The thought had never crossed Cassie's mind. She lifted the latch nervously, but thankfully the door swung open. Another flight of steps appeared before them. The torchlight didn't penetrate much further than the bottom of these.

'It's a deep old cellar,' Matthew remarked. 'Cold too.'

The cold, dank air hit them as soon as they started to descend. Emily shivered.

'I don't think I fancy going down here on my own.'

'Oh, you'll be all right,' said Cassie. 'Come on, we've got to cross this big cellar, then we should reach a door on the other wall.'

The two torchlight beams criss-crossed in the darkness, trying to locate the door. But they had to walk quite a bit further before it appeared, slightly to their right.

On reaching it, they were relieved to find it was standing slightly ajar. Cassie and Becky pushed it, but it was wedged against the stone floor. They all helped push, but it wouldn't budge.

'I think we'll have to lift it up a little,' said Matthew.

This did the trick, but even so, the door made a terrible scraping sound as it opened.

'Hope no one's just above us,' said Emily nervously.

'Look,' said Cassie, shining the torch on to the plan. 'We need to bear right here, then we should come to a passage.'

'This must have been a wine cellar,' Becky remarked, as the children trooped past tiers of empty wooden racks.

The passage was soon reached and Cassie stopped to consult the plan once again. 'This is where our wing joins on to the main building,' she said.

'It's just like a rabbit warren under here!' Abigail declared.

The passage opened out into another large cellar room. Cassie flashed her torch along the wall as they walked, revealing glistening patches of damp.

'Now, this must be the north wall,' she said.

'Is this the door we need to go through next?' asked Becky, as the torch shone on a small, old door.

'No, not according to the plan,' answered Cassie. 'Our door's straight over there!'

'Where does this one lead then?'

Cassie studied the plan and frowned. 'There's no door marked here, and no other cellar rooms north of this one!'

'Well, let's open it!' cried Matthew. 'And solve the mystery.'

But when they tried to open the old oak door, they found it wouldn't budge.

'What a shame,' said Cassie. 'I'd love to have found out where it led.'

'It may not actually be locked,' said Matthew. 'Just jammed.'

When they'd passed through two further large rooms, Abigail asked,

'When are we going to come up again?'

Cassie laughed. 'Don't worry. Not long now.'

Soon her torch flashed across a staircase leading up to the ground floor.

'Thank goodness,' said Emily. 'It's like another world down here. You feel cut off, somehow.'

'When I come back down on my own, I'm going to run so fast I won't have time to think about it!' said Poppy.

'I can't wait for my turn,' said Becky. 'It's going to be so exciting!'

They emerged from the cellar door in single file. It led out into the back lobby of the kitchen area and they were immediately aware of voices and clattering in the kitchens. Washing-up must still be in progress after supper, Cassie thought.

She put a finger to her lips and the children crept through the lobby. It would cause awkward questions if the kitchen staff were to catch them there.

They hadn't far to go before they reached the servants' old back staircase, the first flight of which was sometimes used to get up to the first floor. But, this time, they continued up the second flight, leading to the attic.

'I'm sure this must be out of bounds,' said Emily anxiously.

'It's funny how nobody ever thinks to go to the attics and cellars,' said Cassie.

'Yes,' agreed Becky. 'And I've never heard Miss Wrench say we mustn't.'

Where the cellars had been dank and cold, the attics were dusty and warmish. As soon as she had set foot into the first attic room, Cassie started sneezing. The room was partially lit by a skylight, but as they progressed from room to room, it gradually grew darker and more cobwebby.

Whereas the first room had had a proper boarded floor, now the children were having to pick their way from beam to beam and could really have done with a torch apiece.

When Cassie stopped once more to shine the torch on to her plan, Matthew, who was last of the six, bumped into Abigail and they both overbalanced. Fortunately they landed gracefully and without hurting themselves.

They were now nearly at their exit point.

'I reckon that we are now standing directly above Miss Oakland's room,' whispered Cassie.

'Well at least she isn't there,' Becky whispered back.

'Even so,' hissed Emily, 'we ought to be careful. Those two made a bit of noise falling over!'

As they came out again into electric light, Cassie had to blink hard and wait a few moments for her eyes to adjust to the glare. They were back in the girls' wing, on the staff floor, but were safely concealed while they remained on the attic stairs, as there was a door in front of them, with a glazed panel over it, letting in the light.

'We thought we'd have the start and finish here,' whispered Cassie, 'because we're well hidden.'

'There shouldn't be any problem going past the staff bedrooms on your way to the cellar, because of the staff meeting.'

'Who's going first?' asked Becky.

'It ought to be Cassie – it was her idea,' said Abigail, who perhaps was not as fearless as she seemed.

'Fine,' said Cassie, but with a slight flutter inside. 'Then I can warn you if there are any problems.'

Cassie flew down the steps and turned the door-handle.

'Oh great!' she exclaimed. 'It's locked.'

'Look, Cassie,' said Matthew. 'It's not locked; it's bolted, near the bottom. We're not timing you yet, don't worry.'

Cassie undid the bolt and paused for Poppy to reset the watch. Then she slipped through the door, which was closed quietly behind her by Matthew, and zoomed off in the direction of the stairs to the girls' landing.

She made it to the cellar steps without meeting anyone at all. As she closed the door behind her, the fluttery feeling came back. Now she was on her own, being down in the cellars didn't seem quite such a good idea. It was eerie and she felt a million miles from the rest of the school.

But she knew if she was to have any chance of

winning the race, she would have to get going down here. There was certainly no possibility of running through the attics. So she sped through the maze of musty rooms, not giving herself time to think about shadows in corners or what was lurking behind the next door.

She was very glad to surface again. Even though the kitchens were now quiet, comforting smells still issued from them, welcoming her back to her normal school world.

Her heart bumping, she ran fleetly down the corridor to the back staircase, and took the steps two at a time. By the time she reached the first attic room, she was puffed. The room had darkened along with the sky outside and she needed her torch straight away. She had to slow down once she passed into the rest of the attic rooms on her route, because of the lack of flooring.

Luckily, her dancer's sense of balance stood her in good stead. She felt she must be making good time. *Funny though, my breathing still hasn't settled down after running up the stairs.* She was so fit that she normally regained her breath very quickly, even after very intensive exercise.

As she picked her way across the last of the rooms, a tight hand seemed to be pressing on her chest, and she began to gasp for air. The atmosphere was very close and she began to panic. Her legs had turned to lead; it became a terrific effort to keep them moving at all. *What's happening to me? Why do I keep getting these funny attacks?*

Crossing that last attic room seemed to take longer than the whole of the rest of her journey. As she stumbled down the steps to her friends, she sank down, exhausted.

'Cassie, whatever's the matter?' asked Becky. The friends huddled round her anxiously.

'You haven't seen a ghost, have you?' asked Emily nervously.

'No,' gasped Cassie. 'Leave me a minute!'

'You're going to have to see Matron and the school doctor,' said Emily. 'This is like the attack you had the other day, isn't it, only worse!'

It was too much effort to speak.

'Come back to the room,' said Emily. 'I'll stay with you. I'd rather not be in the race anyway.'

Cassie's breathing was deepening gradually, but now there was a wheezing sound.

'Come on,' said Becky. 'Emily's right.'

'No,' said Cassie. 'I want to stay here and see who wins.'

'Well, let me get you a glass of water at least,' said Emily.

While Emily was getting the water, Abigail set off on her lap of the cellars and attics.

'Good luck!' called Poppy after her.

The glass of water revived Cassie, although she was still audibly wheezing. She persuaded a reluctant Emily to go next, and Becky followed her.

'Abi's got the fastest time so far,' said Poppy, on Becky's return.

'Not for long,' said Matthew. 'I'm going next.'

The girls all groaned. 'Hope the cellar spook gets you!' said Abigail.

Matthew grinned and leaped through the door as soon as Poppy said 'Now!' When he got back a few minutes later, the girls had to admit he had recorded the fastest time.

'It's up to you then, Poppy. Don't let us down,' wheezed Cassie, who was feeling a lot more cheerful again.

'I won't,' said Poppy.

'I'll time you,' said Cassie, taking the stop-watch from her. 'Now!'

'You ought to be in bed, Cassie,' said Becky, after Poppy had disappeared.

'What, and miss all the excitement. No fear! Oh, I hope Poppy wins.'

'Thanks!' said Matthew.

Cassie grinned at him. 'Nothing personal!'

They heard Poppy coming through the last attic room towards them.

'She's making a lot of noise,' said Abigail.

'She's doing an amazingly fast time,' said Cassie, looking at the watch.

Suddenly there was a sickening, splintering crash and a loud yell, from just beyond the doorway to the attic.

'That's Poppy!' cried Emily.

Cassie stopped the watch and they all scrambled up the steps and shone the torch into the attic. Poppy had missed her footing and was stuck, with one leg through the plasterboard which must be

43

part of Miss Oakland's ceiling.

'Oh no!' Cassie groaned. 'This could mean trouble with a capital T.'

'Let's get her out,' said Matthew, yanking Poppy under her arms, 'and scarper.'

'Ow,' moaned Poppy. 'You're hurting my leg.'

'You haven't broken it have you?' asked Emily.

'I don't know,' whimpered Poppy.

They were all suddenly aware of footsteps coming up the stairs.

'Get out of here,' urged Poppy. 'The other way!'

'No, we're not leaving you to face it all on your own,' Cassie gasped.

They turned towards the doorway, as Matthew shone a torch into Miss Oakland's startled face.

'Who is it?' she called.

Matthew went across to her and lit her way back to the group.

'Oh it's *your* foot, Poppy, is it, that's dangling through my ceiling!' said Miss Oakland, regaining her composure. 'What on earth have you all been up to?'

Becky offered her an explanation, knowing that Cassie was still finding it difficult to speak.

'Reviving an old tradition, eh?' said Miss Oakland. 'Have none of you heard of such a thing as asking permission?'

She knelt down to have a better look at Poppy.

'I'll have to get the caretaker to enlarge the hole to get you out. Is your leg hurt?'

'I don't think so. It's my foot that's throbbing.'

'Well, straight to Matron when he's got you unstuck.

I'm afraid I can't feel much sympathy. It's a crazy thing for dancers to be doing, rushing around through dangerous attics. You should all have more sense!

'I'm just glad I wasn't at the staff meeting. I'd come up to my room with a headache.'

'Sorry, Miss Oakland,' said Becky.

'Cassandra, will you stay here with Poppy, while I go and find the caretaker?'

'Yes, Miss Oakland.'

'You look very flushed, Cassandra. You have really been behaving stupidly, all of you! I'll be reporting this to Miss Wrench. Now, the rest of you, get back to your rooms and just hope and pray that Poppy here hasn't fractured anything, or you'll all be in the soup!'

While they waited for the caretaker, Cassie sat close to Poppy. She felt so relieved that the tightness in her chest had relaxed that she hardly thought about seeing Miss Wrench the next day. Even so, she wished she hadn't been asked to stay behind in the attic. She longed for some fresh air.

'Oh, these cobwebs are awful!' she complained.

'I don't mind the cobwebs, it's the creepy things that make them I don't like,' called Poppy.

'It's so stuffy up here,' said Cassie.

'You go, Cassie. You haven't been well. I'll be all right on my own.'

'Oh, no. I'm not risking getting into any further trouble with Miss Oakland. There's one good thing though.'

'What's that?' Poppy asked.

'*You* won the race, not Matthew!'

45

'How d'you make that out? I didn't even finish the course!'

'Near enough. Adding on a couple of seconds for you to reach the door, your time was still faster.'

'Well, that's some consolation for being stuck in an attic with my leg down a hole!' Poppy laughed.

Cassie was swinging her torch aimlessly across the rafters above her head. 'Hey, what's this?' she cried.

'Well, I can't actually get up and take a look, can I?' said Poppy.

'There are some initials carved into this beam!'

She examined them in her torch-light. 'E.A.' she said.

'Do they look old?' asked Poppy.

'There's a date too,' Cassie said excitedly. '3. 12. 71. Oh, wouldn't it be nice to know whose initials they were!'

'It's bound to have been someone who was doing the Unders and Overs,' said Poppy.

'So it wasn't just a tradition in Mrs Allingham's time,' said Cassie. 'It was still being done twenty-odd years ago.'

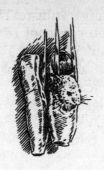

5

Auditions

Miss Wrench's steely eyes swept across the semi-circle of faces in front of her.

'Miss Oakland has told me of a very stupid and dangerous prank you all got up to last night. Cassandra Brown, I might have guessed you'd be among them. Whenever there's trouble at Redwood, it seems you're in the thick of it!'

Cassie hung her head and looked suitably shamefaced.

'And Poppy, I see you have your foot strapped up. Is it injured?'

'No, Miss Wrench,' answered Poppy. 'It's only a little bruised, but Matron insisted on bandaging it up for me.'

'Well, you are very fortunate. This prank could have ended in disaster for any one of you. And I'm sure I don't have to tell you that I don't expect such behaviour from any of you again! Is that understood?'

'Yes, Miss Wrench.'

'Poppy and Abigail, as this is your first year with us, I imagine that you were followers rather than leaders and, as such, your punishment will be less severe than that of the others.'

As she paused, Cassie and Becky exchanged glances.

'You will have litter duty for seven days. You may leave now, while I deal with your friends.'

Poppy and Abigail curtseyed to their Principal, with a look of great relief in their eyes, and got out of the door as quickly as they could.

'Now,' said Miss Wrench, pacing back and forth behind her desk. 'Whose idea was this silly race?' She stopped and glared at the four friends.

Cassie gulped. Should she own up?

'Well?' Miss Wrench demanded.

'Er, it wasn't our idea,' Cassie said, in the uncomfortable silence.

'And whose was it then, young lady?'

'Well, I don't know really. But I do know it's an old tradition of the school. It used to go on fifty years ago, maybe longer.'

'What rubbish!' exclaimed Miss Wrench. 'I know all the traditions of the school and I have never heard anything about crawling through the attics. And I wouldn't mind betting that you're the ringleader of this little escapade.'

'I'm not making it up,' said Cassie quickly. 'Mrs Allingham told us that she did the Unders and Overs as a girl, didn't she, Becky?'

'Yes, that's right, Miss Wrench.'

'The Unders and Overs, you say. Well, I see now where the idea came from.' Miss Wrench sat down. The friends could see that her attitude had softened. 'But this doesn't excuse your foolish behaviour one little bit.'

Cassie crossed her fingers behind her back in the pause which followed.

'You'd better all have a week's detention,' said Miss Wrench finally. 'And let's have no more of this unseemly behaviour. Now be off with you.'

Cassie and her friends didn't need telling twice. Unleashed, they felt a wonderful sense of freedom.

'That was a master-stroke, Cassie,' said Matthew admiringly. 'Bringing in Mrs Allingham.'

Cassie laughed. 'Yes, it saved our skins, didn't it?'

Several times in her tap class, she thought about her good fortune. *Perhaps my luck will hold in the Cinderella auditions*. These were to be held later that same day.

But at that moment, Mr Whistler was putting them through their paces.

'Stop, everyone!' he called. 'You still haven't got that shuffle quite right, most of you.'

He swept the hair out of his eyes impatiently. The class stopped in mid-step and gazed admiringly at him. The boys took him as a role model, for how they would like to turn out when they were older. And the girls – well, the girls just thought he was wonderful.

49

'Rebecca,' he said, beckoning to her.

Cassie could almost hear Becky's heart pounding.

'Would you demonstrate the sequence for the rest of the class? You've such a good sense of rhythm, and your shuffle is spot on.'

Becky went pink with pleasure and, smiling broadly, gave her demonstration. Feeling pleased for her friend, Cassie reflected that this was one form of dance that Becky definitely did enjoy. But whether she would if it were not Mr Whistler taking the class, was another question!

The *Cinderella* auditions were held in the late afternoon, after academic school had finished. Cassie and her competitors had learned a short extract from Cinderella's and the Fairy Godmother's roles, and one by one they danced for Madame Larette, Miss Oakland and Miss Wrench.

As Cassie walked into Studio One for her audition, she wondered if Miss Wrench would still be angry with her for the Unders and Overs escapade. On the other hand, all the girls going in for the leading roles had been involved. All except Celia, that is. Cassie's heart sank at the thought. Celia would be unbearable if she were chosen as Cinderella.

She tried to clear her mind of these dispiriting thoughts as she began to dance. There was some very quick footwork to do, and some difficult jumps. She needed to concentrate.

She started well, but as the dance grew more energetic, the familiar tightness returned to her chest.

Oh no, she thought. As on the previous occasions, she was soon gasping for breath. She kept going longer than she should have done, in order to finish the audition. But her dancing had been wrecked.

She bent over double, holding her knees at the end. Madame swept over to her, in concern.

'Have you the stitch, ma cherie?' she asked.

'No, Madame. I've not been feeling too well. I'm sorry I messed up the audition.'

'These things 'appen. Perhaps a touch of 'flu? You'd better go to bed now.'

Cassie left the studio in tears, knowing without a shadow of doubt that neither of the leading parts would be hers. Her friends made a fuss of her, but out of the corner of her eye, she could see Celia looking as pleased as Punch.

Poppy was to go in next.

'How's your foot?' Becky asked.

'It's still a little sore,' said Poppy. 'But I'll manage, I think.'

It suddenly crossed Cassie's mind that Poppy, too, was handicapped, and wasn't making any fuss about it either. Cassie's breathing had improved again after resting. It was hard to believe there was anything really wrong with her. Perhaps she was getting panic attacks, just when she needed to be on top form. It was very confusing.

While she changed, Poppy came out and Emily went in.

'How did it go?' she asked.

'Could have been better,' answered Poppy, smiling.

51

'I reckon you and I will end up as the Ugly Sisters, Cassie.'

Cassie suddenly felt a whole lot better. *You win some, you lose some,* she said to herself.

'Come on, Poppy,' she said brightly. 'We can be first in the supper queue.'

When they joined Becky in the dining-hall, they joked with her about ending up as the Ugly Sisters.

'You can't be!' Becky cried. 'I've ear-marked one of them for myself.'

'When's your audition?' asked Cassie.

'Seven o'clock,' said Becky.

'Best of luck then.'

'I'm not going to have time to give Hammy his evening run,' said Becky. 'Could you let him out for me, Cassie?'

'Yes, sure. Poppy and I will look after him.'

'Do you feel all right again now?' Poppy asked.

'Yes, I'm fine,' said Cassie. Although her breathing had returned to normal, she actually felt quite drained and light-headed.

'Have you had another funny turn?' asked Becky.

'Yes,' Cassie admitted. 'In my audition.'

'Oh Cassie, you must go to Matron. It might be something serious.'

That's what I'm afraid of, Cassie thought.

'No, it's nothing much,' she said aloud. 'Probably all in the mind.'

'But it would be best to see a doctor, surely?' said Becky.

Poppy shook her head. 'You can't force her,' she said.

'No,' said Cassie stubbornly. 'I'll manage.'

But when she was trying to get to sleep that night, she did wonder if she would have to seek help. The breathing difficulties had come back almost as soon as she lay down. Her three room-mates had been asleep for ages and she was beginning to panic. The room seemed unbearably stuffy. She had to get out!

She slipped into her dressing-gown and slippers and went on to the landing. The movement made her gasp even harder, but it was better to be doing something than suffocating in bed. She went into the bathroom, splashed cold water on her face and had a long cool drink. She sat on a stool, every muscle in her chest, neck and arms straining with the effort to breathe.

Suddenly there was a shadow in the doorway.

'Who is it?' she gasped.

'Emily! What's the matter, Cassie? I heard you get up.'

'I feel so ill, Em.'

Emily knelt down on the floor and put her arms around her.

'Come on, now, Cassie. Just relax and try and breathe more deeply.'

Tears began to trickle down Cassie's cheeks.

'You must promise to go to Matron in the morning,' said Emily.

'No, no, don't make me,' sobbed Cassie.

'Don't cry, it'll make you worse! Why don't you want to see the doctor?'

'Oh, don't you see,' Cassie gasped. 'If they find something wrong they'll throw me out, won't they?'

Emily was silent.

'WON'T THEY?'

'I don't know, Cassie. But your health is more important. You can't go on like this!'

Cassie felt exhausted the next morning. She hadn't dropped off to sleep until the early hours, and even then, she'd had to prop herself up almost in a sitting position. But, once she was up and about, there was no trace of any tightness in her chest.

So when her friends all nagged her once more about going to see Matron, she refused point-blank.

'It might never happen again!' she said to them. 'I'm breathing fine now! It's not as though it's all the time. There can't be anything seriously wrong with me.'

Becky sighed. 'You're stubborn, Cassie Brown. And I still say we need to get to the bottom of this.'

'Are you all ready?' asked Cassie, ignoring her. 'The audition results might be posted up on the noticeboard.'

As they made their way downstairs, they were joined by Abigail and then, less fortunately, Celia.

'Meet your new Cinderella,' said Celia. 'I'm sure I clinched it. Unless Abigail's beaten me to it.'

Despite the fact that Abigail no longer gave her any encouragement, Celia still regarded her as a close friend.

'Well, let's wait and see, shall we?' said Poppy.

Cassie read the results without any expectations, which was a novel feeling. At least it meant that there was no disappointment to follow. She had been given a tiny solo as the chief star among the group of stars which danced in the finale of the ballet. Celia, on the other hand, whose expectations had been so high, was only in the corps de ballet.

'I don't believe this!' Celia shouted. 'There must be some mistake.'

'Come on, Celia,' said Abigail kindly. 'There just aren't enough parts to go round everybody. Your turn will come one day.'

Celia stormed off and the friends began to congratulate each other. Abigail had been chosen to dance Cinderella; Emily was to be her understudy; Poppy, despite her bruised foot, had been give the part of the Fairy Godmother; and Becky was an Ugly Sister.

Matthew came clattering up behind them.

'How did we get on?' he called. When he saw that he was the other Ugly Sister, he whirled Becky round in glee. 'Well done, my facially-challenged sibling!' he crowed.

'What on earth does that mean?' asked Becky laughing.

'Ugly sister, to you,' said Matthew. 'Who's the Prince by the way? Tom and Ojo both went in for it.'

'Ojo,' said Emily. 'I shouldn't think Tom was tall enough.'

'You must be feeling pleased with yourself, Em,' said Cassie, though even as she said it, she took in the look of unhappiness on Emily's face.

'Yes,' said her friend. 'Anyway, must dash. I've got a lot of practice to do if I'm to be good enough for Easter!'

She slipped away from the group and Cassie was left thinking that perhaps Emily was disappointed that she was only the understudy, even though this meant she would dance the leading role in at least *one* of the performances of *Cinderella*. Her attention returned to the group. Matthew was talking.

'Wouldn't it be fun to go down again, perhaps take some tools and see if we could open it?'

'What are you talking about?' asked Cassie.

'You know, that locked door in the cellar,' Matthew explained.

'I don't think any of us knows how to pick locks!' said Cassie.

'Well, I was thinking. It might not be locked, just wedged. I've got a screwdriver I could take down.'

Cassie's eyes brightened. 'Sounds great,' she said. 'Count me in – when can we go?'

'Not yet,' said Becky protectively. 'You didn't get much sleep last night, remember.'

'And we really mustn't get caught this time,' said Poppy.

'Well, I think the Wrench was crosser about us being in the attics,' said Becky. 'They're more dangerous.'

'Even so,' said Poppy. 'Let's not take any chances.'

In the end, the friends chose Saturday afternoon, when most of the school trooped off to the local shops and there was only a skeleton staff left.

'Hurry up, Becky!' called Cassie. 'We're all ready except you.'

'I've just got to finish cleaning out Hammy's cage,'

56

said Becky. 'Here, hold him for me, will you?'

As Cassie stroked Hammy, wishing that Becky would hurry up, her nose began to tickle and she began to sneeze violently.

Becky looked up at her. 'Caught a cold?'

'No, I don't think so,' said Cassie. 'I don't know what's making me sneeze. But just hurry up, Becky!'

At last, they made their way down into the cellars. Emily had refused to come as she wanted to practise and Abigail had needed to go shopping, so only Cassie, Becky, Poppy and Matthew were left of the original six.

They had their torches, the plan and Matthew's screwdriver with them.

'I still say the door's locked,' said Cassie, as they made their way through the warren of cellars.

'Bet you it isn't,' said Matthew.

When they reached it, Matthew prised the door open with his long screwdriver. 'See,' he said. 'Just stuck.'

But Cassie didn't reply. She was too busy staring through the partly-opened door. What stretched ahead, for what looked like a considerable distance, was a tunnel.

'Wow!' cried Becky.

'I wonder if it's safe,' said Poppy.

'The brickwork looks sound,' said Matthew, examining the roof of it with his torch. 'Come on, let's explore.'

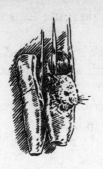

6

Underground

Matthew led the way down the gloomy tunnel, lighting only a small portion of it with his torch. Cassie, just behind him, screwed up her eyes to peer as far as she could. It was impossible to see the end of the tunnel.

'If it leads up into the grounds, we should be able to see a circle of light soon,' Matthew said.

'Or it may come up in a forgotten chapel or something!' hissed Cassie.

'A lot of these old tunnels were blocked off,' said Becky. 'I don't suppose we'll get very far.'

But the four friends went on walking through the tunnel for several minutes.

'Where on earth does it lead?' cried Cassie. 'It must

have been an escape route for someone hundreds of years ago!'

'The brickwork's in very good nick,' said Matthew.

'It's pretty damp and slimy, though, isn't it?' said Poppy.

'You'd be damp and slimy if you were as old as this tunnel,' Matthew quipped.

'Oh look!' called Cassie, craning her neck over his shoulder.

In the torch beam, they could all just make out the shape of a flight of stone steps.

'We've reached the end!' she said. 'Now where will it come out, I wonder?'

They climbed the slippery steps quickly but carefully. There was a turn in them; as they rounded the corner, their torches lit up a brick and stone wall.

'Oh, how disappointing!' cried Cassie. 'After coming all this way!'

'Now we'll never know where it leads,' Becky sighed.

'I don't know about that,' said Matthew.

'No,' said Cassie. 'We can't give up now!'

The girls reported their findings to Abigail and Emily later that evening.

'Oh, I wish I'd come with you,' said Abigail. 'I didn't expect you to find anything so exciting!'

'Nor me,' said Emily. 'I didn't even think you'd get the door open. Can we go with you next time?'

'Of course you can,' said Cassie. 'We're trying to figure out where the end of the tunnel is. It must be in the grounds somewhere. If you look at the plan here and trace a line northwards from the north wall, where the door is, it crosses the lawns.'

'Oh yes, I see,' said Emily. 'But does the tunnel go in a straight line?'

'I'm not sure it was directly north. We'll have to take a compass down with us,' said Cassie. 'But there weren't any bends in it, fortunately.'

'I've got a compass somewhere in my locker,' said Abigail.

'Great,' said Cassie. 'Let's go down again next Saturday afternoon. It's too risky in the evenings.'

Cassie wasn't to know that the planned exploration of the tunnel would have to be put off on her account.

She had still been getting wheezing symptoms every night in bed – some nights worse than others – but had been relatively free from problems in the daytime since the day of the audition. But on Thursday, after a very restless night, she found herself having a bad attack of breathlessness in the middle of Miss Oakland's ballet class.

They were just practising the grand jeté, a step which called for a good deal of stamina. Cassie was forced to tell the ballet mistress that she was feeling ill.

'Go and lie down until lunch-time,' said Miss Oakland. 'And if you're no better by then, go along to Matron.'

Cassie got changed and walked slowly back to her room. The stairs were the real killer. She had to pause on each one, to get enough breath to climb the next.

Lie down, she thought. That was the last thing she

wanted to do. She propped herself up on her bed, and started reading.

When her friends came to see her at lunch-time, the symptoms had abated.

'Come on then,' said Becky. 'I'll go with you to Matron.'

'I'm not going,' said Cassie flatly. 'I'm feeling much better again. It always passes off.'

Becky and Emily looked at each other and sighed.

'We've got to do something about you,' said Becky. 'If you won't go and get help, I'll just have to bring it to you.'

'What d'you mean?' said Cassie. 'You're not to tell Matron or anyone. Promise!'

'I promise,' said Becky. 'That's not what I was thinking of.'

She would say no more until she returned at four o'clock, with a very large book from the library.

'What's that?' asked Cassie.

'*Your Family's Health,*' Becky replied. 'I'm going to look up your symptoms.'

Cassie laughed, despite herself. 'You're going to end up as a doctor, not a vet!'

After poring over the book for the next twenty minutes, Becky announced her diagnosis.

'It's asthma, I think, Cassie,' she said.

Cassie was stunned. 'But that's awful,' she said. 'It's the sort of thing that old people get.'

'Not really,' said Becky. 'It says here that it's become very common in children. And it also says in the majority of cases it can be treated successfully.'

'Does that mean it can be cured?'

'I don't know,' answered Becky. 'You'll have to see a doctor. You can't go on without medication. It could damage your heart!'

Cassie went very white. She couldn't be an ostrich and bury her head in the sand any longer. The school staff would have to know. Now, there seemed little chance of a dancing career, or of remaining at ballet school.

'All right, you win,' she said quietly. Emily squeezed her hand. 'I'll go and see Matron.'

Becky and Emily went with her. Cassie was installed in bed in sick-bay, to await the doctor's visit the following day.

'It doesn't seem long since it was me in that bed. And I got better,' Becky said encouragingly.

Cassie smiled wanly at her two close friends. 'You needn't stick around being cheerful,' she said. 'I've got a good book. You'd better get back to your homework.'

When the doctor arrived at nine o'clock the next morning, Cassie's chest had tightened up again. She had slept badly, despite bolstering herself up with four pillows.

He was able to hear her wheeziness with his stethoscope and measure her out-breath with a special tube she had to blow into.

'Well, there's no doubt in my mind,' said the doctor, after he'd asked Cassie a few questions. 'You have a condition called asthma.'

Cassie was thankful that Becky had already

prepared her for this diagnosis. Otherwise, she was quite sure she would have burst into tears.

The doctor prescribed two inhalers for her, a blue one and a brown one.

'Now, the blue one will give you relief when you have symptoms, but it won't prevent the attacks. Even so, I want you to take it four times a day, until you see the chest specialist I'm writing to for an appointment.'

'What about the brown one?' Cassie asked.

'Now, that is a preventative medicine. You must take two puffs twice a day, morning and night. But unfortunately, it won't begin to have an effect on you for about twenty-eight days.'

That sounded a long time to Cassie. Long enough to get thoroughly out of practice.

'The specialist will tell you more. He might want to change the inhalers even. And he may suggest what's triggering the attacks.'

There was a lot to think about. She stayed in sick-bay, under Matron's supervision, for two days. By the end of that time, she was terribly bored and, when Miss Eiseldown came to visit her, Cassie pleaded with her to be allowed back to classes.

'Are you sure you feel well enough?' asked Miss Eiseldown.

'Yes, I'm fine. In between attacks I feel quite normal. Just a bit tired.'

'Madame has asked me to have a word with you,' said her housemother gently. 'About the tour.'

Cassie's face fell. 'I suppose it's bad news.'

'Yes, I'm afraid so. While your health is unstable,

we think it would be foolish to take you to France. And I'm sure your parents will agree. Don't take it too hard, Cassandra. There will be other tours, don't worry!'

There was worse to come. When Cassie went along to the next *Cinderella* rehearsal, she was demoted to the corps de ballet and Celia was given her small solo as a star in the final Act. As she watched Celia learning it, Cassie tried to switch her mind to something else. The tunnel!

Her friends had told her they would wait to go down again until she was better. Perhaps they would be able to go this coming Saturday . . . But her mind kept coming back to her disappointment.

The ballet was beginning to take shape now. Abigail was proving to be a very strong Cinderella; her personality came shining through, even in rehearsal. Emily, as well as being her understudy, had a lovely solo as Spring, one of the Four Seasons, in the first Act, but Cassie thought she seemed to have lost some of her old sparkle.

There was a murmur of surprise in the room when Mr Whistler walked in. He hadn't had anything to do with rehearsals up till now.

'Ah, Mr Whistler,' said Madame. 'Just the man we need!'

She explained to Becky and Matthew that the tap teacher had choreographed a special pas de deux for the Ugly Sisters.

'I think it will be fun!' said Madame. 'You two 'ad better go into the other studio with Mr Whistler, *n'est-ce pas?*'

65

Becky looked delighted and winked at Cassie on her way out.

Using the new inhalers made a difference to Cassie. She had a further two attacks over the next few days, but they did not get so severe. Bedtime was still a trial, however, and it was often past midnight before she could drop off to sleep.

In the end, the friends had to put off their tunnel visit for a week. The following Saturday, Emily and Abigail were very keen to be included. They were quite astonished by the length of the tunnel, when they reached the end.

'I wonder where we are?' said Abigail as they stopped at the blocked-up exit.

Cassie and Matthew joined the group of friends. They had been measuring the distance of the tunnel door from the far wall of the cellar room.

'What d'you think?' Cassie asked.

'It's amazing!' said Emily.

Cassie sat on the bottom step and, while Emily held the torch for her, plotted the tunnel door on her plan. Then Abigail showed her the compass reading, and she drew a line from the door, stretching out across the grounds.

'Now we just need to know how long the tunnel is,' said Cassie. 'We can measure it on our way back.'

She trundled the measuring wheel they had borrowed from the maths room back along the tunnel and recorded the distance.

'A hundred and forty-nine metres!' she exclaimed.

'Are you all right, Cassie?' Emily asked, when Cassie started gasping a bit in the cellars.

'Yes, I'll just have a blast on my inhaler. I'll be OK.'

'Well, stay here and have a rest for a few minutes. There's no rush.'

But Cassie quickly grew impatient. 'I want to get outside and find out where this tunnel leads!'

'It's going to attract too much attention if we all start taking measurements in the grounds,' said Becky. 'Why don't you go back to the room, Cassie, while Poppy and I do it?'

'No, I want to be there,' said Cassie. 'I wouldn't miss this for the world.'

Becky sighed. 'OK. You and I then. The rest of you had better stay at a discreet distance.'

But first they had to study the plan, in order to find a point on the ground floor of the school building which corresponded to the door to the cellars. This point turned out to be a drain-pipe on the back wall of the girls' wing.

From there, Becky and Cassie pushed the wheel in an easterly direction along the north wall until they knew they were standing parallel (although on a higher level of course) to the cellar door. Then, using Abigail's compass, they struck out north-north-west away from the school, across the lawns.

'Do you see where we're heading?' Cassie puffed.

'The woods?' said Becky. 'By the way, Cassie, I'm glad I've got you on your own for a bit. I wanted to talk to you about Emily.'

'Emily? Why?'

'Haven't you noticed, Cassie? She's gone so *thin* and there are awful dark rings under her eyes.'

'I hadn't noticed,' Cassie admitted, feeling a flood of guilt. She had been so caught up in her own problems, she hadn't really looked at Emily for weeks.

'What d'you think is the matter with her, Becky?'

'I don't know. She goes off by herself all the time. Perhaps she's working too hard. Or brooding about her father. You're the only one she'll talk to, Cassie. Ask her.'

'I will,' Cassie promised. She broke off to check the wheel. 'We're nearly there,' she said.

Both the girls looked ahead, expectantly. The ruined folly loomed before them, a darkening silhouette against the redness of the late afternoon sky.

The girls stared at one another. 'The folly!' exclaimed Becky. 'Does the tunnel come up right inside it, d'you think?'

Cassie took the wheel as far as she could, until the fallen stone-work prevented her.

'I think it must. We've another two and a half metres to go. That would take us comfortably inside, I think.'

With great excitement, the two girls scrambled up the steps of the tower and began waving frantically at the others, who were some way off across the lawns. An answering wave came, and very soon their friends had joined them at the folly.

They all squeezed into the base of it, some standing on large stone blocks.

'There must be a hatch in the floor somewhere,' said Cassie, looking about her.

'There's so much stone-work lying about,' said Matthew. 'I expect we'll have to shift it.'

The friends cleared away the smaller-sized debris and with a joint effort, managed to move two of the heavier stone blocks.

As they pushed aside the last one, Cassie shouted. They had uncovered a square iron door with a large ring handle.

'Fantastic!' Matthew hissed. He took the ring, along with Cassie, and yanked hard. The door swung upwards, nearly hitting Poppy and Becky, who jumped back in surprise.

'Who's got the torches?' shouted Cassie.

Becky offered her one, which she shone down the gloomy cavity.

'There's some steps!' cried Cassie.

Matthew was already lowering himself through the hatch. He took the torch and went down, and one by one, the friends followed him. They were quickly brought to a halt by a brick and stone wall – the other side of the very same wall they had encountered at the end of the tunnel.

'Well, here's a job for us!' said Matthew. 'It'll take quite a few lunch-hours!'

'What, you mean, knock it down?' cried Emily.

'We only need to make a hole big enough for us to get through,' said Cassie. 'We can borrow some tools from the CDT block.'

On the way back to school, as the excitement of

69

their find began to wear off a little, Cassie remembered what Becky had been saying to her about Emily. She took a good look at her friend, who happened to be walking beside her. *Yes, Becky's right. Emily is looking very thin and tired.* Cassie mentally kicked herself again for not noticing before now.

'I don't seem to see much of you, these days,' she said to Emily.

'No, I suppose not. Are you feeling better now, Cassie?'

'Yes, much. Although I still get asthma at night quite a lot. But what about you, Emily?'

'What about me?'

'I mean, are you feeling OK?'

'Yes, shouldn't I be?' Emily answered defensively.

'It's just that . . . well, you look as though you've lost weight, that's all.'

'Oh, don't worry about me,' said Emily. 'I needed to go on a diet. I was too fat for Cinderella. I could do with losing a few more pounds yet.'

'Oh no!' cried Cassie. 'No more. You're looking really thin. Honestly, Em. You were never fat to start with.'

'Who are you kidding?' said Emily. 'Anyway, dancers all need to watch their weight.'

'But we burn up so much energy, dancing,' said Cassie. 'We need lots of good food to keep up our stamina.'

Emily shrugged, as if to say, Do what you want and I'll do what I want.

'How are things at home?' Cassie asked.

70

'Oh, I haven't thought about them for weeks,' said Emily. 'Now, I must dash. I've wasted quite enough of my practice time for one day.'

Cassie gazed after her retreating figure. There was something very strange happening to Emily. And she was going to make it her business to find out what it was.

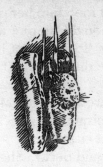

7

A Vanishing Trick

Over the next couple of weeks, the friends put into effect their plan to make a hole in the wall at the end of the tunnel. They took it in turns to go to the folly in small groups of two or three, so as not to arouse suspicion. Cassie was often not well enough for the extra exertion, much to her annoyance. She always liked being at the centre of things. And Emily seemed to have lost all interest.

Cassie tried again and again to get Emily to talk to her, but it was hopeless. She was always going off on her own to practise. The mealtimes she didn't skip altogether were almost token efforts. Watching her carefully, Cassie noticed something she hadn't noticed

73

before. Emily put food into her mouth and chewed it but, when she thought no one was looking, she put her napkin to her lips and spat it out. She would no longer talk in the dining-hall. She just sat there in a sort of dream.

'Do you think we should tell Miss Eiseldown about Emily?' Cassie whispered to Becky one morning, on their way to ballet class.

'No, we can't,' said Becky. 'She'd never forgive us.'

'I suppose you're right,' said Cassie. But she felt deeply troubled about her friend.

Ballet class was getting more and more difficult for Cassie to manage, as her sleepless nights accumulated and took their toll on her stamina. Miss Oakland tried her best to be understanding; Cassie's asthma had been explained to her. But Cassie could see how frustrated she was that one of her star pupils should be so incapacitated. Miss Oakland only just managed to keep her feelings disguised.

On that particular morning, it became obvious to her friends that Emily was struggling to get through her exercises too. Cassie wasn't really surprised. On the amount that Emily was eating, she couldn't have had much energy at all.

Miss Oakland quickly spotted Emily's difficulties. Cassie could imagine the thoughts going through the ballet mistress's mind: another of her best students going to pieces! What on earth was happening to this class?

Miss Oakland vented all her pent-up frustrations on Emily.

'What's the matter with you this morning?' she asked harshly.

'I . . . I don't know, Miss Oakland,' said Emily.

'You look like a sack of potatoes. Put some attack into your dancing!'

It wasn't long before the ballet mistress stopped the class again. Emily had stumbled during her pirouettes.

'Emily,' spat Miss Oakland, 'I think you had better do a lot of extra practice this week.'

'But I do, Miss Oakland,' cried Emily. 'I practise all the time.'

'Well, it's obviously not enough,' said Miss Oakland. 'Make sure your standard has improved after the half-term holiday, or I'll not have you in this class!'

Cassie was amazed that Emily remained dry-eyed throughout this onslaught. In the changing-room after class, she tried to comfort her friend, but Emily stayed aloof and didn't encourage her attentions at all.

Perhaps the holiday which was coming up would help Emily to sort herself out, Cassie thought. She would probably thrive again on home cooking and wouldn't get so much opportunity to practise. A rest from Redwood could do her nothing but good.

Certainly half-term benefited Cassie a great deal. Her parents had been worrying a lot about her asthma, and took her to see the family doctor on her first day home. He said nothing different from the school doctor, and Joy and Jake Brown resigned themselves to waiting until Cassie's appointment with the chest specialist.

Cassie enjoyed the fuss her parents made of her.

She got plenty of rest, food and fresh air and by the end of the week, she felt like a new girl. She hadn't had an asthma attack for five days now, and had had long, delicious sleeps in her own comfortable bed.

'Well, you're looking more like our Cassie now,' said her mum. 'You looked awful when we picked you up.'

'I've never seen you with such dark shadows under your eyes,' said Jake.

But although Cassie was so much better physically, her parents could see that she was still quite low-spirited.

'What's worrying you, Cassie?' asked Joy.

'Well, what use is a dancer with asthma?' Cassie blurted out. 'And you know how fussy they are at Redwood about medical conditions.'

'Look how Becky has got on!' Joy countered.

'She was a special case. The doctor said ballet training would help her full recovery.'

'Perhaps ballet will help your asthma,' Jake suggested.

'I doubt it! Exercise seems to bring on attacks.'

'Now don't give up yet, Cassie,' said her dad. 'We don't know what the specialist will say. And there has been a huge improvement in you this week.'

'Yes,' said Cassie, 'away from ballet school.'

When she got back to Redwood on Sunday afternoon, Cassie was fully expecting to see the same improvement in Emily. But when her friend walked into the room, she felt shocked by her hollowed cheeks and extreme pallor. Emily looked worse than ever.

Cassie could contain herself no longer. 'Emily!' she burst out. 'You look really ill. Let me take you to Matron.'

'Why should I need Matron?' answered Emily, with a touch of defiance.

'Oh, please come with me, Em. Remember how I kept putting it off. I see now how foolish I was. Just pretending the problem wasn't really there.'

'I'm not like you,' said Emily. 'I'm not ill.'

'Well, you look it,' chipped in Becky. 'Cassie's right. You should go and see someone – Miss Eiseldown, if not Matron.'

'Stop going on at me!' cried Emily, suddenly losing her cool. 'I'm not staying here a moment longer.'

She dumped her belongings on her bed and fled the room.

'Shall we go after her?' asked Cassie.

'No, it's pointless,' said Becky. 'She's got to want help.'

They saw Emily again at supper-time, but she refused to sit with them.

'You're looking so much better, Cassie,' Becky remarked over her chicken and roast potatoes.

'Yes, I feel it,' said Cassie. 'Perhaps it's all been a bad dream!'

'How about a midnight feast tonight?' Becky whispered to the group of friends.

'Yeah!' breathed Cassie. 'Sounds good to me!'

77

'I've got lots of bars of chocolate and crisps from home,' said Becky.

'We can pool what we've all got,' said Cassie. 'Are we going to have it in our dormitory?'

'No, I've got a better idea,' said Becky. 'How about the folly?'

'Yes!' Poppy broke in enthusiastically. 'We could celebrate getting through the tunnel wall. Cassie wasn't with us when we broke through.'

'Are you coming, Abi?' Cassie asked.

'I sure am,' said Abigail. 'Wild horses wouldn't keep me away!'

'Can you sneak out without Celia noticing?'

'I'm getting masterful at it,' Abigail replied.

'I'll go and ask Emily,' said Cassie.

'You're brave,' said Becky. 'She'll probably bite your head off.'

Cassie shrugged. 'It's worth a try anyway.'

She approached Emily's table, where she was sitting alone, and outlined the plan to her.

'Do you want to come, Em?'

'Why should I want to cram myself full of chocolate?' said Emily.

'You don't have to eat anything,' Cassie pleaded. 'Just come with us for the fun of it.'

'No thanks,' was her answer. 'I want an early night.'

After supper, Becky got Hammy out of the wardrobe and set him loose.

'Didn't your mum and dad notice him missing last half-term?' Cassie asked.

'Of course they did,' said Becky. 'They thought he'd escaped, so I had to hide him in my bedroom over the holiday.'

'Oh, poor Hammy!' cried Poppy. 'He'll begin to think the world is a wardrobe!'

'He doesn't mind,' Becky replied. 'As long as he's fed and he gets a little scamper about.'

Cassie watched Hammy's antics in the bedroom, without really taking them in. Her mind was on Emily, who had gone off to practise, as usual.

Becky and Poppy were kneeling on the floor with Hammy, giving him tubes to run through. Cassie was the only one facing the door, but she was too deep in thought to register anything when Celia walked in without knocking.

Fortunately, Becky had her wits about her and trapped Hammy in a tube as soon as she heard the door open.

'What are you two doing on the floor?' Celia asked curiously.

'Oh, just trying to make a 3D shape with tubes,' Becky answered.

'I didn't know we had to do that for maths homework!' Celia exclaimed.

'It isn't homework,' said Becky. 'Just my own idea.'

'Oh, I see, Miss Einstein,' said Celia. 'I was looking for Abigail.'

'Well, she's not here,' snapped Poppy.

'OK, OK, I only asked. See you,' said Celia, disappearing fast.

The girls waited for Miss Eiseldown to put her head

round the door after lights out, making sure everyone was in bed. Once they heard her high heels receding, they hurriedly got dressed again, donning coats and hats as the night, although fine, smelled cold. Abigail joined them as they made their way down to the back entrance of the wing, with Poppy in front as look-out.

The air was cool and crisp on their faces as they spilled out on to the grounds. They walked briskly away from the school, hoping that no member of staff might be looking out at that moment. Crossing the lawns safely, they were just approaching the folly, when Abigail laid her hand on Cassie's shoulder.

'We're being followed!' she hissed.

Cassie turned and peered back across the grass. She could just make out a figure coming towards them.

'It's not tall enough for a teacher,' she whispered.

'It must be Celia,' said Abigail in disgust. 'I was sure she was asleep, but she must have been foxing.'

'She's sure to tell on us,' whispered Poppy. 'What shall we do?'

A plan came to Cassie in a flash. 'Quick! Follow me!'

The friends followed her into the folly.

'Oh, I get it!' said Becky. 'Down the tunnel.'

'A good vanishing trick, eh?' said Cassie. 'Just make sure last one down covers the hole with the big stone.'

The children had used this to hide the entrance ever since they found it, not wanting to share their secret with any of the other Redwood students.

'She'll never guess!' Poppy tittered.

'And the beauty of it is, I'll be back in bed before she's finished looking for us,' said Abigail, starting to go down the steps to the tunnel.

'She'll think she's been seeing things,' said Becky, following her.

Once the stone was back in place, they climbed through the hole they'd made in the wall.

'Aren't we going to have our feast?' asked Becky in a disappointed voice.

'We ought to get back,' said Poppy.

'No need for us all to,' said Abigail. 'As long as I'm back in bed, Celia won't do any more nosing.'

'Oh, it's a shame you'll have to miss it,' said Cassie.

'I don't mind,' said Abigail. 'I've enjoyed the excitement. See you tomorrow!'

With that, she hared off down the tunnel. The friends watched the light from her torch bobbing along until it disappeared.

'Let's move further down,' suggested Cassie. 'Celia might hear echoes if she's around the folly.'

The girls found a dry patch of floor to sit down on for their feast.

'Celia didn't have a torch, did she?' asked Poppy.

'No,' said Becky. 'She won't see much.'

'I'd love to be up there, just to see her face,' said Cassie.

Finding it too cold to hang about for long, the friends contented themselves with a quick nibble, taking a chocolate bar each to munch on the way back through the cellars.

Their journey back to Room 12 was uneventful, although they were careful as they passed Celia and Abigail's room. Cassie could hear the murmur of voices within and imagined to herself the sort of strange conversation that must be going on. She chuckled inwardly.

When she got into bed, Cassie realised that not once during that evening had she thought about her worries with regard to staying at Redwood. But now, of course, as she tried to settle herself down for sleep, everything came flooding back. There were two voices in her head, having a bitter argument. One said, *You'll have to leave ballet school. You're too ill ever to be a dancer.* While the other one argued, *You're stubborn enough, determined enough to win through. Don't give up!*

In the midst of this inner argument, she remembered Emily and how awful she looked. *Perhaps we shall both have to leave Redwood – two of the best students of the year!*

And now Cassie felt that all-too-familiar tightening of the tubes in her lungs. She had forgotten to take her bedtime inhalers. That was it. But even after using them, the asthma attack stayed with her and kept her awake for most of the night.

She felt despondent the next morning. She was too tired and shaky to attempt ballet class and even had to be excused from her morning lessons. After resting all morning, she revived. When Becky came into the room at lunch-time, Cassie greeted her quite chirpily.

'Hi,' said Becky. 'Feeling better?'

'Much,' Cassie answered. 'I feel like some fresh air and stretching my legs.'

'We can go for a walk after lunch,' said Becky. Once they had eaten, the girls decided to walk across to Mrs

Allingham's. Becky had been a few times on her own, to keep an eye on Tinker, but it was some time since Cassie had been.

It was a relief for Cassie to talk to the old lady about her problems. It made her realise how much she missed her mum in term-time, when there was something wrong, as now.

Mrs Allingham's face puckered in concern. 'I'm really sorry, Cassandra. But you mustn't feel too down about it. People can rise above all sorts of terrible handicaps. I'm a great believer in mind over matter.'

'What does that mean?' Becky broke in. She had Tinker curled up on her lap, purring his head off.

'Oh, you know, if you believe it hard enough, you can make anything happen. Each one of us has so much more potential inside us than we ever dream we have.' She laughed. 'I'm getting quite philosophical in my old age.'

'So do you mean that if I believe I'm going to be a vet, I will be one?' asked Becky.

'Not without a lot of hard work as well,' said Mrs Allingham with a smile.

Cassie sighed. 'I wish Emily weren't working so hard,' she said. 'She looks dreadful, doesn't she, Becky?'

Becky nodded.

'Isn't she allowing herself any recreation?' asked the old lady.

'No,' said Cassie. 'And she's even worse now she's been chosen as Cinderella's understudy.'

'You must always keep a balance,' said Mrs Allingham.

'All work and no play makes Jack a dull boy!'

'My mum says that!' said Becky.

'Do you think she would come over to see me? I could have a word with her.'

'No, I don't think she would. She won't have anything much to do with us at the moment, because we told her to go to Matron.'

'Why did you do that?'

'Because we think she's ill. She hardly eats a thing.'

'Has she lost weight?'

'She's very thin,' said Becky.

'I'd have thought Matron would have noticed when she weighed her after half-term,' said Mrs Allingham.

'I think Emily avoided it,' said Becky. 'She hid herself away when we all queued up for weighing.'

'And is Emily still worrying about her family?'

'I'm sure she is,' said Cassie, 'though she denies it. And she was worried about the money for the tour.'

'Well that's easily fixed, at least,' said Mrs Allingham. 'I'll increase the bursary to cover the tour expenses. I'll speak to Miss Wrench today.'

'Oh, thank you,' Cassie cried. 'That'll be one weight off her mind.'

'I wish I could do more,' said Mrs Allingham. 'I feel very disturbed by what you've told me. Emily, I suspect, has become anorexic.'

'That's quite serious, isn't it?' asked Cassie.

'Yes, indeed. It can be life-threatening in some cases. Whether Emily agrees or not, you must speak to Miss Eiseldown or Matron. As soon as you get back to school.'

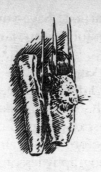

8

Escape!

When Cassie and Becky got back to their room, Emily was there, sorting out her books for the afternoon's lessons. Cassie decided to tackle her straight away.

'Emily,' she said, 'we've been over to Mrs Allingham's and happened to get talking about the tour. And guess what! She's putting your bursary up to cover the cost. So you don't need to worry about it any more.'

'I don't want more of her charity,' Emily said stiffly.

'Oh Em, it's not like that, and you know it. You *won* that bursary,' Becky said.

'We're going to see Miss Eiseldown about you later,' said Cassie firmly. 'Will you come with us?'

Emily looked startled. 'Save yourself the trouble,' she said. 'She's sent for me anyway. I've got to go and see her at four.'

'What about?' asked Cassie.

Emily shrugged. 'I don't know really. Although Miss Oakland's probably been complaining about me. I made a bit of a mess of things in class this morning.'

She was ready before Cassie and Becky, and went on ahead to the geography lesson.

'Will it all come out now?' Becky said.

'We can't take any chances,' said Cassie. 'Emily's so good at denying anything's wrong. We'll go too.'

At four o'clock, as Emily made her way along the landing in the direction of the stairs, her friends caught her up.'

'We're coming with you,' said Cassie.

'I don't want you to!' said Emily. 'Go back to the room.'

She tried to rush on ahead of them, but they stayed abreast of her, even though it made Cassie rather breathless.

'Why don't you leave me alone?' cried Emily.

'Because we're your friends,' panted Cassie.

'And we're worried about you,' said Becky.

When Miss Eiseldown answered their knock, she looked very surprised to see three girls standing there.

'Come in,' she said. They followed her into her bed-sitting room, which was arranged tastefully, with a few pretty prints and ornaments and a couple of dried-flower arrangements.

'I appreciate your coming with Emily, to give her

moral support,' she said tactfully to Cassie and Becky, 'but I really think I need to talk to her on her own.'

Cassie had anticipated this. 'Before we go, Miss Eiseldown, Becky and I want to tell you something that Emily might not.'

'Oh?' asked their housemother, raising her eyebrows. 'And does Emily know what you're going to tell me?'

'Yes,' answered Cassie. 'She . . .'

'Stop it!' broke in Emily. 'It's none of your business, Cassie.'

'Don't get upset, Emily,' pleaded Miss Eiseldown. She turned to Cassie. 'I really think it better if you go now.'

'We *must* tell you,' Cassie insisted. 'It could be a matter of life and death.'

Emily had begun to shake visibly and Miss Eiseldown looked at her carefully before nodding to Cassie to proceed.

'You see, we think . . . we're *sure* that Emily's anorexic. She eats hardly anything. That's why she's got no energy for her dancing. And then she pushes herself to practise all the time.'

'Is this true, Emily?' Miss Eiseldown asked gently, again scrutinising the girl's face.

'Of course not, I've just been dieting a bit that's all. I'm still too fat for Cinderella.'

Miss Eiseldown was by now looking very worried indeed.

'From what Cassandra has told me, coupled with the reports I've been getting from your dancing teachers, it looks as if I'd better take you to Matron straight away.'

'I don't know what everyone's getting so worried about,' said Emily. 'I'm just a bit tired, that's all.'

'Well, I'd like to check your weight records and let Matron have a look at you.'

Cassie and Becky were allowed to accompany their friend, who had gone very quiet. When they got to Matron's room, Miss Eiseldown quickly explained the situation.

Matron looked closely at Emily's eyes and picked up one of her hands. Her own small hand easily encircled Emily's painfully thin wrist.

'Mmm, her pulse is on the weak side.'

'May I see her weight records?' the housemother asked.

Matron found the appropriate book and showed Miss Eiseldown Emily's height and weight records.

'There's a steady, though small, loss of weight here,' she commented. 'But there's no entry since half-term. Why is that?'

Matron looked flustered and took the book to look at herself. 'I . . . I don't know. If Emily was here, she should have been weighed. I can't understand it.'

'Perhaps we could pop Emily on the scales now?' suggested Miss Eiseldown.

When the two women read the weight which the scales registered, they looked at each other with a shocked expression on each of their faces.

'She'll have to come into sick-bay,' said Matron. 'I'll feed her up, don't worry. The poor thing's skin and bone. There's nothing that Cook's milk-pudding won't cure.'

Miss Eiseldown didn't look entirely convinced. 'I think we should contact the doctor,' she said.

'Well, that's up to Miss Wrench,' said Matron. 'But I shouldn't think it's necessary at the moment.'

Miss Eiseldown went off to report the matter to the Principal, while the friends settled Emily into sick-bay. They were as kind to her as they knew how, fetching her a walkman, tapes, books and magazines. But Emily didn't respond and they knew she was still angry with them.

As the days passed, Cassie and Becky were frequent visitors to sick-bay. Each day they hoped they might see a return of the sparkle in Emily's eyes, but nothing seemed to change.

'Are you eating anything?' Cassie asked one evening.

Emily shook her head. 'I don't feel like food. Those milk puddings Matron keeps bringing me make me feel sick as soon as I look at them.'

'Isn't there anything you fancy?' asked Becky. 'I'm sure Matron would get it for you.'

'No,' said Emily quietly. 'I seem to have got out of the habit of eating. I'm sorry for all the trouble I've caused. But I just can't help it!'

'Oh, don't talk like that, Em,' cried Cassie. 'We're your friends. We just want you to get better.'

Emily looked so sad at that moment that Cassie flung her arms round her and hugged her. She was shocked when she felt how bony Emily had become.

Her pyjamas hid the worst of her thinness.

The door opened and Matron bustled in, looking flustered again. 'Off you go, you two. Miss Wrench wants to speak to Emily.'

Cassie and Becky bobbed a curtsey as they passed their Principal just outside the sick-bay door. There wasn't enough time before lights out to return again that night, so they had to wait until morning to go back to sick-bay, in order to find out what Miss Wrench had said.

They found Emily in floods of tears.

'What's happened, Em?' cried Cassie, sitting on the bed beside her.

'M . . . Miss Wrench has phoned for Mum to come and collect me.'

'Well, I suppose that's sensible really,' said Becky. 'Your mum can look after you and get your family doctor to help and everything.'

'No, she's *suspending* me until I'm completely recovered. She said she's not having an anorexic pupil in her school. And even if I do get better, she doesn't guarantee she'll have me back.'

'I'm sure she doesn't mean it,' said Cassie, thinking the opposite. 'She's just trying to shock you into eating.'

'Something's got to make you eat!' Becky exclaimed. 'Or you'll die!'

Emily dried her eyes. 'Tell Matron I'll have some soup.'

'That's the idea!' said Cassie. 'It's in *your* hands, Emily.'

The friends sat with her as she sipped at the bowl of vegetable soup Matron had got for her. She took it down painfully slowly, as if every spoonful were a torment. She only managed a quarter of it, but Matron looked pleased all the same.

'There now,' she said. 'That's a good girl. Once you're home with Mum, you'll be as right as rain.'

Emily's expression darkened. 'Mum's got enough to cope with, without having to coax me to eat.'

'Don't you worry,' said Matron kindly. 'That's what mums are for. I'll help you dress and then these two friends of yours can help you pack. Your mother's arriving at lunch-time.'

Cassie and Becky had to leave Emily to put the finishing touches to her packing, when the bell went for morning classes.

All through ballet class, Cassie could think of nothing else but her friend. It had even stopped her worrying about her own future at the ballet school. Now Miss Oakland knew about Cassie's asthma, she rarely picked on the girl for making mistakes. But on this particular morning, Cassie seemed worse than usual.

'Did you have a bad night, Cassandra?' she asked, as they moved from the barre into the centre.

'Not really, Miss Oakland,' Cassie answered.

'Well, stop day-dreaming, then, and put your mind on your dancing.'

She sighed heavily. 'Goodness knows who's going to be the understudy for Cinderella now Emily's out of action!'

Cassie would have been the obvious choice if she had been well. Poppy had too big a part as the Fairy Godmother.

When Cassie and Becky got back to Room 12 at the beginning of the lunch-hour, they found Mrs Pickering sitting on Emily's bed, among her cases and bags, looking very anxious.

'Miss Wrench said Emily would be here waiting for me,' she said, 'but I've seen no sign of her.'

'Have you tried the bathroom?' asked Cassie.

'No, would you look for me, Cassie?'

Cassie went across the landing and returned quickly. 'She's not there,' she said. 'We'd better check all the bedrooms. She may have gone to talk to someone.'

Privately, Cassie thought this unlikely, but went off to do it anyway, accompanied by Becky.

'I wonder where she's got to?' Cassie said.

'She was so upset, it makes you wonder,' Becky replied. 'And she didn't seem keen on going home.'

The search along the landing produced neither Emily, nor any clue to her whereabouts, and so they had to break the news to her mother.

'Was Emily very upset that she'd been suspended?' asked Mrs Pickering.

'Yes, dreadfully,' Cassie answered. 'And she still looks really ill.'

'It's all that woman's fault,' said Mrs Pickering, making for the door. 'I'm going to give her a piece of my mind.'

As luck would have it, Cassie and Becky saw Emily's

mother a little later, as they crossed the hall after their lunch. She had just come out of Miss Wrench's study and she looked furious.

Cassie ran up to her and asked if there were any news of Emily.

'No,' said Mrs Pickering. 'She should never have been left unsupervised, the state she was in. And that stupid woman . . .' she waved her hand back towards the study. 'She won't bring the police in to look for Emily. Says the staff will find her – there's no cause for alarm.'

'She probably doesn't want the publicity,' said Cassie.

'I'm sure you're right,' said Mrs Pickering. 'The reputation of the school comes before finding my poor Emily! Well, I'm not taking any more of this nonsense. I'm going straight to the police station.'

'Good luck!' Cassie called after her, as she strode away towards the door.

Cassie and Becky both had to go to orchestra practice and so didn't get much chance to talk to their friends about Emily until supper-time. They invited Abigail, Matthew and Tom back to their room after the meal, to carry on the discussion.

'The police are here!' said Matthew excitedly, as they let the boys in. 'I've just seen two detectives talking to Miss Eiseldown and there were several uniformed policemen in the grounds!'

'Miss Wrench *will* be pleased,' said Becky.

Cassie had run across the landing to look through the bathroom window.

'Oh yes!' she called. 'I can see two of them heading for the woods.'

'They'll probably call in on Mrs Allingham,' said Becky.

'That's a point,' said Cassie. 'Emily could have gone there.'

'Mrs Allingham would have been in touch with the school by now,' said Matthew. 'No, I don't think she's there.'

'Well where is she?' cried Cassie in exasperation.

At that moment there was a knock on the door. The friends looked at one another for a moment, stupefied. Then Cassie started pointing under her bed and the two boys scrambled under it, as she called.

'Just a minute!'

When she opened the door, Miss Eiseldown was standing there with two detective constables. They both wore dark suits and shiny black shoes.

'DC Peters and DC Jones want to ask you a few questions about Emily,' said their housemother, ushering the two men into the room. She put two chairs together for them, and the girls sat on Poppy's bed, facing them.

'Now, which of you girls have seen Emily today?' asked DC Peters.

'Only Becky and I,' Cassie answered.

'And your name is?'

'Cassandra.'

'OK. And when was the last time you saw her?'

'About eight twenty-five. We had to go to our first class. Emily was still packing.'

'In here?'

'Yes, we'd brought her up from sick-bay.'

'And how did she seem?'

'Very weak and upset.'

'About the suspension?'

'Yes, and I've got the impression she didn't want to go home.'

'I see. Did Emily take any of her belongings with her?'

'Oh, I haven't looked,' said Cassie.

She and Becky went over to Emily's bed, where her suitcase and various carrier bags still lay.

'She's definitely taken her coat,' said Cassie. 'And a big duffle bag she often uses.'

'Anything else?'

'I think her blanket's gone,' said Becky. 'She has a pretty patchwork blanket she throws over her quilt. I noticed she'd rolled it up with her bags.'

'Well, thank you,' said DC Jones. 'If you notice anything else missing, let Miss Eiseldown know immediately. That's all for now, I think.'

DC Peters nodded in agreement, and Miss Eiseldown showed them out.

'All clear,' Cassie called under her bed.

Matthew and Tom crawled out. 'I've been dying to sneeze,' said Matthew.

'And I've been dying to scratch the sole of my foot,' said Tom, desperately untying his shoe laces, to get at it.

'Oh, hold your noses everyone,' said Poppy.

'I don't know how you can joke, when Emily's

95

gone missing,' said Cassie accusingly.

The others went quiet.

'She's probably somewhere in the school still,' said Becky. 'I really can't imagine her going far. Perhaps she just couldn't face her mum and wanted a little breathing space!'

'Let's go and look for her!' cried Cassie. 'I can't bear doing nothing!'

'The police will search for her a lot more thoroughly than we could,' said Poppy.

'That's right,' Abigail agreed. 'I bet she'll be back with us within the hour!'

The girls spent the rest of the day talking about, and waiting for news of, Emily. But after supper there was still no sign of her. Cassie felt very worried.

Becky and Poppy still seemed hopeful that she'd be found before bedtime. Becky had just gone to open the wardrobe to get Hammy out for his evening run, when Abigail popped her head round the door.

'Do you mind if I join you?' she asked.

'Of course not,' said Cassie. 'Come in, though I warn you, I'm not very good company.'

'I just had to get away from my room,' said Abi. 'Celia won't leave me alone, since our vanishing trick.'

'It must have been a great puzzle to her,' said Poppy.

'She keeps asking me all these awkward questions.'

'Does she still follow you about?' asked Poppy.

'Yes, all the time. I told her I was going to the Common Room to put her off the scent.'

Hammy started dashing about, hopping over the children's feet.

'Come on, Hammy, Hammy,' Poppy coaxed, when the little hamster went under her chest of drawers.

'Just leave him,' said Becky, 'he'll come out in a minute!'

The door swung open and everyone groaned.

'Celia!' shouted Abigail. 'You're following me again.'

At that moment, Hammy shot out from under the chest of drawers and headed straight out through the open door.

'Oh no!' shrieked Becky. 'After him!'

'Come on, Celia,' Abigail said, as she followed Becky. 'It's your fault Hammy's escaped.'

'Don't see why,' said Celia, hanging back. 'Nobody told me they'd got a pet in the room.'

'You've got to help. I shall never forgive you if you don't.'

This did the trick and Celia was soon up at the front of the chase, with Becky and Cassie. Becky had spotted Hammy running down the stairs, so the girls followed suit. Celia got excited and shouted back to Abigail that they'd spotted him.

As Cassie went chasing off down the staircase, it struck her she shouldn't be wasting time on Hammy, when she could be looking for Emily. But Poppy was right, really. The police would be a lot more thorough than they could be.

Still, she longed to do something. A thought occurred to her. *Perhaps Emily had gone off with her dad?*

She suddenly became aware of her surroundings. They were in the main building, near the library. Celia was racing ahead, making a great deal of noise.

There was no sign of Hammy.

Celia and Becky stopped in their tracks when they saw Miss Wrench around the corner.

'Oh no!' Cassie breathed.

'Now there's no chance of catching Hammy!' said Becky sadly.

Celia had been too near the corner and going too fast, to stop in time. She blundered right into the Principal, and came to an awkward halt.

'I'm . . . I'm very sorry, Miss Wrench,' she stammered.

'Detention for you, Celia!' was all that Miss Wrench would say to her. 'And what are all you girls doing out of your wing? You know the rules. Order marks for all the rest of you!'

'Sorry, Miss Wrench,' each one of them mumbled, with a curtsey of apology.

'There are problems enough in the school at the moment without you girls adding to them.'

As Miss Wrench stalked off down the corridor, Cassie again thought of Emily. Now Emily and Hammy were *both* missing. Would they be found in time?

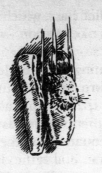

9

Hammy Pops Up

Becky shook Cassie awake the next morning. 'He hasn't come home!' she moaned.

Becky had left the door ajar all night, in case Hammy found his way back. She had left the wardrobe open too and a bowl of his favourite nibbles in his cage.

'I'm going to leave our door propped open while we're away at lessons, just in case!'

'Don't worry, Becky. He's sure to pop up somewhere.'

Cassie didn't realise then how true her words would turn out to be.

She had slept badly. Her breathing wasn't back to

normal during ballet class, which made the jumping section – the steps of elevation – virtually impossible for her to execute.

During her morning academic lessons, she felt tired and depressed, worrying about Emily. So when Hammy popped up, she was taken completely by surprise. It was in their maths lesson. Miss Eiseldown was writing some equations on the blackboard, so she didn't see him. But several of the class did. Fortunately all of these particular children knew about Becky's hamster, so didn't raise the alarm.

Hammy strolled along the window-sill to the right of the classroom. The nearest desk was empty, so no one could actually reach him without getting up. Cassie could see Becky straining to keep herself in her seat. It would have been pointless to get up – Miss Eiseldown would have turned round and seen Hammy.

'What can we do?' whispered Cassie.

'Absolutely nothing,' Becky whispered back. She watched her pet as he plopped down on to the empty desk and from there on to the floor.

'Now someone might catch him,' she hissed. She turned round in her seat and put a finger to her lips, warning the rest of the class to keep quiet.

But Hammy successfully evaded the hands which reached down to grasp him, and got across to the far corner of the room, again out of reach.

Miss Eiseldown, aware of a greater degree of movement among her pupils, swung round and peered at them.

'Anything wrong?' she asked.

Several children shook their heads.

'There seems to be a . . .' began Ojo from the side of the room nearest Hammy. He stopped in mid-sentence, after a warning kick under the table from Matthew.

'Yes, Ojo . . . there seems to be a what?' Miss Eiseldown prodded him.

'Oh, yes . . . a . . . a draught!' cried Ojo, triumphantly.

'I wasn't aware of one, Ojo,' Miss Eiseldown replied. 'But if you want to move further forward, there are several spare places.'

Cassie and Becky were willing Hammy to stay on the floor in the corner out of sight till the end of the lesson. Then they might find an opportunity to get him.

In the event, he did move again – this time right under the teacher's desk. Fortunately Miss Eiseldown had her back to the class when he moved, and once he was under her desk, she couldn't see him, at least while she was standing up.

'Oh don't sit down, Miss Eiseldown,' whispered Becky, with her fingers crossed.

The girls spent another nerve-wracking half-hour, expecting the teacher to sit down at every moment. At the end of the lesson, Hammy was still at large and undetected and the girls hoped that Miss Eiseldown would be moving to another classroom.

Becky deliberately spilled the contents of her pencil case on the floor and the two of them spun out the time as much as possible picking everything up.

'You two will be late for your next lesson if you're not careful!' the teacher chided.

'We shan't be a minute,' Becky called. 'Don't wait for us, Miss Eiseldown.'

'Oh, *I'm* not moving,' said Miss Eiseldown. 'I have a fourth year class in here next.'

As she spoke, she pulled her chair out from the teacher's desk, and made to sit down.

'Miss Eiseldown!' Becky cried sharply.

The teacher stood up again hurriedly. 'Whatever is it, Rebecca?' she asked.

'I . . . I just saw a man at the window. Over there!'

'A man?' cried Miss Eiseldown, moving over to the window. Becky seized her opportunity, but as she stretched out her hand to grab Hammy, he shot from under the desk and out of the door.

'I can't see any sign of a man,' said Miss Eiseldown, turning back to them. 'Rebecca, what are you doing under my desk?'

'Oh, my pencil rolled over here, I think.'

'Well, I don't know who or what you saw, but you'd better both be off or you'll be in trouble. Oh, and by the way, if you watch the Midlands regional news tonight, there's supposed to be an item on Emily.'

As Becky was telling her friends about her close encounter with Hammy, at the lunch table, they were all startled by a piercing scream from the direction of the kitchen. Cook came puffing into the dining-hall, her white hat bobbing among the tables of children. She was brandishing a large rolling-pin.

'A mouse! A mouse!' she shrieked as she weaved through the tables.

'Are you thinking what I'm thinking?' Cassie said to Becky.

Becky had already got to her feet, hoping to be the first to reach her hamster. But dozens of children were already in hot pursuit of the mouse by the time she reached Cook.

Hammy could occasionally be glimpsed, running frantically in zigzag patterns across the hall.

'There he is!' called Cassie, pointing. Hordes of children chased after him, frightening the little creature right out of the hall. Once Cassie and Becky got through the double doors, there was no sign of Hammy anywhere, and groups of children were standing about, looking indecisive.

The girls had to wait several hours for their next sighting of him. First, there was afternoon school, followed by a *Cinderella* rehearsal.

Madame Larette was in charge today. She announced that they would miss out Emily's Spring Fairy solo altogether. 'I 'ave decided not to give Emily's parts away just yet. *Ma pauvre* Emily will be back soon,' she said with more confidence than Cassie felt.

Cassie thought to herself that if Madame had seen Emily's physical condition before she had disappeared, she wouldn't be thinking in terms of her being better in time for Easter. But at least Madame's words gave her a new feeling of hope.

She was glad on that day she had nothing very important to do in the rehearsal of *Cinderella*. She could cope with being on the back row of the corps de ballet without having to think very hard about what she was doing.

After supper, the friends rushed up to the Junior common room and switched on the television, just in time for the regional news. Reports of fires and floods were followed by a feature on school children's playground rhymes.

'They're not going to say anything about Emily,' said Becky, looking at her watch.

But suddenly, there was Emily's photo staring at them from the screen, followed by an image of policemen scouring the grounds of their school. The newscaster said the police were appealing for anyone who had seen Emily to get in touch with them immediately.

'It brings it home to you, somehow,' said Cassie, once they had switched off the set. 'Oh, Emily, if only we could find you!'

'The police are doing their best,' said Poppy gently.

As if on cue, the two detectives appeared. Miss Eiseldown was with them.

'They'd like to ask you some more questions,' she said to Cassie and Becky. 'Come with us up to your room.'

When they got there, the door was still wedged open.

'Don't you want your door closed?' asked Miss Eiseldown, once they were all inside.

'Oh, no thanks, Miss Eiseldown,' said Becky quickly. 'It gets a bit stuffy in here.'

Cassie wondered fleetingly what they would do if Hammy decided to choose that moment to pop back into Room 12.

'Now girls,' said DC Peters. 'I've brought a tape recorder this time. Better than relying on this.' He tapped his forehead.

'It won't put you off, will it?' asked DC Jones, the younger of the two. He grinned at them disarmingly. Switching on the tape, he announced, 'March the tenth. Interview with Redwood Ballet School students.'

He clicked off the tape again. 'What are your full names by the way?'

'Cassandra Brown and Rebecca Hastings.'

He repeated their names into the recorder and then went on. 'Also present: DC 2152 Peters, DC 3365 Jones, and member of staff, Miss Eiseldown. Interview commenced at nineteen hundred hours.'

'Tell us all you can about Emily's state of mind just before she disappeared,' said DC Peters.

So Cassie, with help from Becky, described Emily's family problems and her recent over-working and weight loss.

'Do you think things had got worse at home?' the detective asked.

'Since Christmas, yes definitely,' Cassie answered. 'Emily told me that the bouquets her dad had sent her had caused a lot of trouble with her mum.'

'Did Emily mention her father to you at all this term?'

'Hardly at all,' said Cassie.

'Do you think it was possible he was secretly in touch with her?'

Cassie's thoughts began to jumble. Emily had become very secretive. Perhaps her dad *had* been writing to her, even seeing her?

'I don't know,' she answered truthfully.

'It's unlikely,' Miss Eiseldown broke in. 'Students are not allowed out of school unaccompanied.'

'But I bet they manage to slip out now and then without getting caught!' said DC Jones, smiling at the girls.

Cassie blushed. Her own recent escapades came flooding back. At least she had never gone out of the school grounds, though.

'One more thing,' said DC Peters. 'Did Emily give any hint that she might run away?'

'Not really,' said Becky. 'She looked too weak when we left her in the room, anyway.'

'She couldn't have been kidnapped, could she?' Cassie asked suddenly.

'We can't rule it out,' said the detective. 'There were no signs of a scuffle. If she went off with someone, it was of her own free will, I'm pretty sure.'

'A stranger in the building would always be stopped and questioned,' Miss Eiseldown countered.

'But Emily disappeared during morning lessons, I believe,' said DC Peters. 'When presumably most of the staff are busy teaching.'

Cassie could see what was running through their minds. Emily's father may have come into school secretly and abducted his daughter.

'Anything else you can think of, girls?' DC Jones asked. When they shook their heads, he spoke into the recorder: 'Interview concluded. Nineteen twenty hours.' He switched the machine off with a dull click.

'Off the record,' said DC Jones, 'watch out for the reporters. They're buzzing round the main doors. One of them might even find a way in unnoticed.'

Cassie saw that Miss Eiseldown had flushed. 'Why can't they leave us alone?' she complained. 'None of us wants to talk to them about Emily.'

'Well, if they get too much of a nuisance, let us know,' said DC Peters.

The girls crossed over to the window to peer out at the drive, which they overlooked. The policemen were right. Quite a crowd of reporters had gathered there.

'I don't understand why it's drawn so much interest,' Miss Eiseldown commented.

'They sense a story. Something a bit different from the usual MISSING GIRL – POLICE HUNT kind of thing.'

'How do you mean?'

'Well, the fact that Emily is at a ballet school makes it more glamorous for a start. Then, of course, they may have got wind that she's anorexic. The two things together – well, you can see what I'm getting at, can't you?'

'Yes,' said Miss Eiseldown, with a worried frown. 'Yes, I can.'

She turned to the girls as she was ushering the two detectives from the room.

'Mind you don't speak to any of the press,' she urged.

But at breakfast the next morning, it became apparent that someone must have spoken to the press. Matthew had sought permission to run down to the paper-shop in the village and brought back with him a copy of one of the leading tabloid newspapers. He lay it out before his friends on the breakfast table.

On the front page, in large block letters was the headline:

STARVING BALLET GIRL MISSING FROM TOP SCHOOL

'Oh goodness,' said Becky. 'Miss Wrench won't like this one little bit.'

'Some of the press are very good at twisting the truth for sensational effects,' said Matthew. 'Let me read the column aloud to you:

Mystery surrounds the disappearance on Thursday of baby ballerina, Emily Pickering, a boarder at top dance establishment, Redwood Ballet School. It is alleged that Emily, twelve, is a victim of the eating disorder, anorexia nervosa, and was suspended by the Principal of the school, Miss E. Wrench, just before her disappearance.

Her mother, Mrs L. Pickering, is outraged by the Principal's heavy-handed treatment of her daughter. She claims that no medical attention had been sought for Emily and that, despite her very weak condition, she was left unsupervised to wait for her mother to collect her.

'I should have been informed about Emily's problem long before it reached this stage,' said Mrs Pickering last night. 'The school has been negligent.'

Meanwhile, police are making a thorough search of the neighbourhood. They are not ruling out abduction at this stage.

'Oh I hope Emily's all right,' said Cassie. 'She could starve to death, couldn't she?'

'And my poor little Hammy,' said Becky with a sigh.

Cassie fell silent. She could understand Becky's concern, but at this moment, she couldn't share it. Emily was gone. That was what really mattered. Hammy's escape, Cassie's own health problems, and the question-mark hanging over her future at Redwood were no longer important to her. She closed her eyes and willed herself to imagine where Emily was.

At first she saw just a jumble of light and shadow. Then a shape began to emerge: Emily's figure, surrounded by darkness. There was just a tiny source of light which lit up the patchwork blanket she was wrapped in. Then the image faded, with Cassie no wiser as to where Emily was. Was it just imagination she wondered? Or was Emily really huddled somewhere under her blanket, all alone in the darkness?

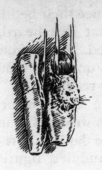

10

What The Papers Said

That evening, the friends watched the television news again. Emily's mother appeared, to make an appeal to Emily to come home.

'Wherever you are, whatever you're feeling, Emily, do come back. Just phone me, and I'll be there. And if anyone's with her, please, please let Emily make a phone call, just so I know she's safe.'

Cassie went to sleep with Mrs Pickering's words ringing in her ears and woke up next morning, surprised to find she had experienced no tightness or wheeziness in the night. When Miss Eiseldown came in to make sure they were all awake at seven, Cassie asked her if there had been any developments since their bedtime.

'No, none that I've heard, Cassandra,' Miss Eiseldown replied. 'But we mustn't give up hope. Emily is probably quite safe somewhere. She'll get in touch when she's ready.'

Cassie knew in the pit of her stomach that her housemother was wrong. The image that had come into her mind the day before re-surfaced even more strongly. The huddled figure; the blanket; the darkness. Cassie knew without any doubt that Emily needed help. And the longer the police took to find her, the more desperate her need.

'She's starving to death,' Cassie muttered, without realising she had spoken aloud.

'Now, now,' said Miss Eiseldown, putting a comforting arm round her. 'You've been reading that silly headline in the paper. Emily's a sensible girl. No harm will come to her.'

Before she got dressed, Cassie said a quick silent prayer for Emily's safety and asked for help in finding her.

'I wonder what Miss Wrench and the staff thought about that awful item in the paper?' said Becky.

'They must be fed up with all the publicity,' Poppy answered. 'I mean, it doesn't do the school's image one little bit of good, does it?'

'No,' said Becky. 'I really think Redwood is going to get a bad name.'

'You don't think they would close it down, or anything?' said Poppy, suddenly worried.

'Oh, I shouldn't think so,' said Becky. 'But there's

bound to be a few questions asked.'

'Miss Wrench will probably get the blame, as she's the Principal and she suspended Emily and everything.'

'But it's not just *her* fault,' Cassie broke in. 'We all saw what was happening and didn't do anything about it till it was too late. The ballet staff must have noticed how thin she was too.'

'She'll never forgive herself if anything awful's happened to Emily,' said Cassie. 'And neither will I.'

'Don't feel guilty, Cassie,' said Becky. 'It's not our fault.'

With all the anxieties about Emily, Cassie had completely forgotten that it was their Easter assessment that day. This was the assessment made by a panel of ballet staff who watched the students go through their normal class-work.

It wasn't as nerve-wracking as an exam, for they took the assessment in a group, not individually. But it was even more important for, each year, several girls were asked to leave because they hadn't reached the required standard. New girls like Poppy were invited into the school the following September after audition to fill the empty places.

Fortunately Cassie felt in better physical condition than previously. Her asthma had not been troubling her the last couple of days. She forced herself to concentrate on her dancing, pushing down her anxieties about Emily. It wasn't easy, however, as her overall mood was one of gloom. You needed a bright spirit to dance with sparkle.

Perhaps they will make allowances for me, Cassie thought to herself when she had finished a difficult enchainement of steps. But really she knew it was too strict a regime for any allowances to be made. *Look how Miss Wrench treated Emily!*

She glanced across in the Principal's direction, and was unnerved to find those steely eyes staring at her. Each member of staff sat straight-backed, with a notebook and pencil in her hands, making notes on the students.

Cassie swung her concentration back to her footwork. It was the batterie section. She was performing a sequence of entrechats, which called for swift, small beating of the feet together. After this, came the harder cabriole, a jump in which the dancer extends one leg and beats the other leg to it, while still in mid-air. Cassie's legs had no bounciness in them at all, but she managed the beat, despite it. She was very relieved when the class was over, as were her fellow-students.

They spilled out into the changing-room, making a terrific din. Cassie was definitely the quietest of the crowd, which was an unusual role for her. Even if she passed this assessment, Cassie's future was insecure. What the chest specialist had to say was crucial in determining her fate.

'You know,' said Becky, untying her pink satin ribbons, 'you've been better the last few days, haven't you?'

'Yes,' agreed Cassie. 'It's funny really. You'd think all the worrying about Emily would make me worse.'

114

'That's what I thought too. Perhaps we should remember what else happened a few days ago?'

'How do you mean?'

'Hammy escaping, of course,' said Becky impatiently. 'How could you forget?'

'Hammy?' said Cassie, none the wiser.

'I'm going to the library later, to look at a few medical books. I think I may be on to something, Cassie.'

Cassie shrugged. She didn't know what Becky was getting at, and she couldn't be bothered to think about it right now.

The next lesson was music, right after their morning break. Mr Green was teaching them the traditional song, 'Scarborough Fair'.

As he stood in front of them, encouraging them to pronounce the words clearly, Cassie thought he looked rather like a fish. They were learning the song without the piano at first, often repeating phrases which didn't meet with Mr Green's approval.

Something yellowish caught Cassie's eye to the left of the music teacher. It was Hammy on top of the upright piano. She quickly elbowed Becky and nodded in the hamster's direction, still singing loudly. She saw Becky go pink.

Hammy looked perfectly healthy. He must have been finding plenty to eat in his travels around the school. Cassie wondered if he'd dared to go back to the kitchens, after Cook had chased him with her rolling pin.

If Mr Green decided to start accompanying the

children on the piano, all would be lost. At the end of the song, Becky's hand shot into the air.

'Yes, what is it, Rebecca?'

'Mr Green, I'm not sure of that bit in the middle. "Remember me to the one who lives there." Could we go over it a few times please?'

'Yes, certainly, Rebecca,' said Mr Green, beaming. Such concern for accuracy was quite unusual in this class.

Becky and Cassie stared at Hammy, while they went on singing, willing him to move off his cheeky position on the piano. But he didn't budge. By now, all the others had seen him too, and there were a few submerged titters.

'Now I think we've got the hang of it,' said Mr Green.

'Help me, Cassie!' Becky hissed in her ear.

Cassie's natural dramatic tendencies came to the rescue.

'Oo-ooh!' she yelled, doubling up and rolling on to the floor. She glanced up at Becky and winked, before moaning loudly once more.

Mr Green came rushing up to her. 'Oh dear, oh dear,' he said, sweat appearing on his forehead. 'Fetch Matron, one of you! Quickly!'

Obligingly, four of the class went charging off in search of Matron.

'What is it, Cassandra? Are you in pain?' he asked, kneeling down beside her.

'Tummy,' Cassie gasped. 'Terrible pain.'

'Oh dear. Now just calm down the rest of you. Give her a bit of space!'

The others formed a pretty tight circle round Cassie and the kneeling music teacher, offering Becky the opportunity to get over to the piano and Hammy. But Hammy didn't want to be caught just yet. As soon as Becky got close to him, he fled, bouncing on the piano keys before landing on the floor.

'I don't think this is the time for tinkering with the piano, Rebecca!' cried Mr Green. 'I'm surprised at you. You should be with your friend.'

Becky saw the hamster run out of the room and reluctantly gave up the chase.

Not surprisingly, Cassie made a miraculous recovery once she'd been taken to sick-bay, telling Matron it must have been trapped wind.

'It wasn't anything to do with your asthma was it?' asked Matron.

'No, no, nothing like that,' said Cassie. 'I'm feeling tons better. I must have eaten too much breakfast that's all.'

'Well, you'd better stay in here today, so I can keep an eye on you.'

Cassie remonstrated, but Matron was adamant. She wasn't going to be blamed for letting *another* sick girl go wandering about the school unattended.

Cassie was fuming by the time Becky came to visit her at lunch-time, with a large book under her arm.

'Look what you've got me into!' she cried.

'Sorry,' said Becky. 'And it didn't even work. I still haven't caught that wretched hamster.'

Cassie laughed, forgiving her friend instantly. 'What's that book you've got?'

'Something very interesting,' said Becky. 'I've been reading all about allergies.'

'Like hay fever and that sort of thing?'

'Yes, that's right,' Becky replied. 'I bet you didn't realise that most asthma attacks are triggered by allergies.'

'No, I didn't.'

'Often things like house-dust, which of course you can never completely get rid of. But a lot of asthmatics are allergic to animals – especially pets which are in the house. Their hairs give off something which you breathe in, and hey presto, you start wheezing.'

'Oh, now I see what you were getting at earlier about Hammy escaping,' said Cassie.

'Yes, while Hammy's been out of our room, you haven't had an attack, have you?'

'No,' said Cassie, with sparkling eyes. 'And I was fine at home as well!'

'We've solved it,' cried Becky, jumping up and down on the bed, and giving Cassie a big hug. 'You won't have to leave Redwood after all!'

'But what about Hammy?' Cassie suddenly asked. Her question hung in the air, as Matron came in just then, tut-tutting at Becky.

'You're getting too boisterous, Rebecca. Cassandra needs a little peace and quiet. Off you go; leave her to rest now.'

Becky had to obey and Cassie was left with the afternoon stretching before her with nothing to do. She begged some magazines from Matron and

118

pleaded with her for so long to let her get up that at last, at four o'clock, she gave in and let Cassie go back to her own room.

She opened the door, expecting to find the others doing their homework, but instead Becky and Poppy were talking to a strange man. Cassie wondered if he was another detective on the case, as he was dressed in a dark suit.

'This is Emily's best friend, Cassie Brown,' Becky said to the man.

Cassie looked at her enquiringly.

'This is Mr Pickering, Cassie. He wanted to meet Emily's friends.'

Memories of what the police had said about abduction came back to Cassie's mind.

'How did you know which room was hers?' she asked suspiciously.

'Oh, a bit of detective work,' he said. He was a handsome man, thought Cassie, but was going grey at the temples and had a lot of worry-lines on his face. As he looked at her out of eyes just like Emily's, she felt sorry she had sounded suspicious.

'Look, it's been hard for me to come here,' he said. 'I don't want anything to do with the staff. They might tell my wife I've been here.'

'How did you know about Emily?' Becky asked.

'I heard it on the news,' he said, putting his head in his hands. He looked very upset and guilty. 'It's all my fault,' he said.

The girls looked at one another, not knowing what to do. He roused himself. 'All I ask of you is to let me know as soon as you hear anything. Here's my phone number.'

He handed Cassie a piece of paper with a Birmingham number on it. She took it and nodded, but he clutched at her hand.

'You must swear not to give that number to anyone. All of you must swear.'

His intensity made all three girls feel uncomfortable, but they did as he asked.

'I must go,' he said, getting to his feet. 'Remember, don't tell anyone you've seen me.' His face had become secretive and hidden, after the earlier burst of emotion.

Cassie and her friends were relieved when he had gone.

'I wish we didn't have to keep it a secret,' said Becky.

'I know what you mean,' said Cassie. 'But, for Emily's sake, I think we must.'

Cassie and her friends settled down for an early night. The three of them felt exhausted. 'It's driving me mad that we can't really *do* anything to help Emily,' said Cassie.

'I know,' said Becky, pulling up her quilt.

The room went quiet. Cassie was thinking.

'I've got an idea,' she said suddenly in the silence.

'Oh, Cassie,' groaned Poppy, 'you woke me up!'

'Come on, spill the beans,' said Becky.

'Well, we can't do anything for Emily but we *can* do something for the school. It's been getting such awful publicity since Emily disappeared.'

'What's your plan?'

'Do a charity stunt and invite the press. Then they'll be able to write about Redwood in a good light.'

'But what sort of charity stunt can you think of?' asked Becky. 'We'd have to get Miss Wrench's approval.'

'Of course,' said Cassie. 'She'll agree to this, I'm sure!'

'What?' asked Becky.

'Tell you in the morning,' Cassie replied mysteriously. 'I want to sort out the details in my head first. But I know which charities to give the money to, the RSPCA and research into anorexia.'

'That's a brilliant idea, Cassie,' said Becky. Cassie snuggled down under her quilt. The darkness was lifting – she could feel it. She knew that she was not going to get asthma that night. If only Emily could be found tomorrow!

'When I catch Hammy,' Becky whispered sleepily, 'I'll keep him in Abi's room – if we can persuade Celia, that is. Then you won't get asthma again.'

'Thanks, Becky,' Cassie murmured and fell asleep.

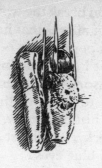

11

Back To The Cellars

Cassie didn't want to wake up. She was having a lovely dream about Emily.

'What's this idea of yours?' Becky hissed into her ear, shaking her awake none too gently. 'I've been trying to guess half the night.'

Cassie stretched her whole body, from the tips of her fingers to the ends of her toes.

'A tap-dancing marathon,' she said.

'Wild!' exclaimed Becky. 'Let's ask Mr Whistler about it – we're having him this afternoon.'

'No, let's go and see him first thing. We need to get it under way as soon as possible.'

When they told him their plan, he was full of enthusiasm.

'We could try and break the world record,' he said.

What was best of all was that he offered to go and ask Miss Wrench's permission.

'That was the bit I was dreading,' Cassie admitted later, when the lessons were over for the day. 'She's much more likely to agree to the charity idea if it comes from Mr Whistler anyway.'

'Yes,' agreed Becky. 'He'd just have to look at her with those dreamy blue eyes . . .'

'I don't think Miss Wrench would notice,' Poppy laughed.

'When do we do this tap marathon, do we *all* have to keep on dancing for hours?' asked Becky.

'No, we'll have teams and change over every hour or so,' Cassie explained. 'We'll have to do it right through the night.'

Poppy groaned.

'It sounds great,' said Becky.

Cassie looked at her watch. 'We'd better go down for supper.'

As they walked along a lower corridor of their wing, a gold-coloured blob streaked past them.

'Hammy!' yelled Becky, forgetting caution and sprinting after him.

Cassie and Poppy followed, hoping that they wouldn't run into any members of staff.

Hammy led them down the steps towards the cellar, vanishing round the door at the bottom, which stood ajar.

'That's funny,' said Cassie. 'We closed it last time we were down here.'

'Perhaps the caretaker comes down sometimes,' puffed Poppy.

'Have you lost him?' called Cassie to Becky, who had come to a standstill a little way ahead of them. Becky came back over to them at the door.

'It's too dark to find him,' she said. 'We'll have to go back for a torch.'

'I'll go,' said Poppy.

'Thanks,' Becky replied. 'We'll stand guard by the door, in case he decides to come out again.'

When Poppy had gone, Cassie began to feel edgy. The gloom of the cellars, as she stared out from the doorway, made her feel uneasy. She shook herself and tried to think about Hammy.

'He could come out the other end,' she said to Becky, 'if he was very clever!'

Poppy returned with her torch and they went into the first cellar. As Becky flashed the torch round the room, looking for her hamster, Cassie's feeling of uneasiness grew. *It can't be the darkness now*, she thought. *What is it?*

They walked on into further cellar rooms. When the torch flickered across their tunnel door, Cassie gasped in surprise.

'It's open!' she cried. 'Someone must have found the tunnel.' Her heart began to pound.

'Oh, don't say the caretaker's found it,' Becky groaned. 'It wouldn't be half so good, if it wasn't just our secret.'

'Give me the torch,' Cassie demanded, with an urgency in her voice. She squeezed through the doorway. The other two followed her.

'Do you think Hammy might be down here?' asked Becky.

'Sh,' said Cassie. 'I can hear something.'

When they stood silently, a low moaning noise could be heard from further down the tunnel.

'Is it the wind?' asked Poppy with a shiver. 'It sounds eerie.'

But then another, quite different sound reached their ears – a high-pitched squealing, which was very close.

'I'd recognise that squeak anywhere,' cried Becky, grabbing the torch and flashing its beam up and down the tunnel.

She quickly located Hammy, who was sitting not ten metres in front of them.

'Now be a good boy!' Becky implored, advancing on him slowly, but purposefully.

For once, Hammy behaved himself and waited for his owner to gather him up.

'Got you, you little rascal,' she murmured to him.

Cassie took the torch back from her impatiently and broke into a run, taking her friends by surprise. They had to put on a spurt to keep up with the torch's pool of light.

'Emily!' Cassie began calling. 'Emily! Emily!'

She strained her ears for an answer, but the sound of her own blood rushing through her head drowned out anything else. Just as she conjured up the image of Emily wrapped in her blanket, as she had seen it in her daydream, the real Emily came into view. And indeed, she was sitting wrapped up in her patchwork blanket, propped up against the side of the tunnel, pinpointed by the torchlight, but nonetheless surrounded by darkness.

The friends threw themselves down beside her.

'Emily, are you all right?' cried Cassie.

She seemed pitifully weak. Her cheeks were chalk white and her eyes were closed.

'She must be alive!' said Cassie. 'I heard her moaning.'

She grabbed Emily's hand and rubbed it, calling her name repeatedly.

Emily's eyes opened with a struggle.

'Cassie,' she whispered hoarsely, but then lapsed once more into semi-consciousness.

'Get help!' cried Cassie. 'I'll stay with her and keep trying to bring her round.'

'We'll have to take the torch,' said Poppy.

'Hang on,' said Becky. 'Emily's probably got one with her.'

Emily's duffle bag, a couple of books and an empty water bottle lay beside her, along with a small torch. Becky picked it up and tried it.

'No good,' she said. 'Batteries have run out.'

'Don't worry, I'll be fine. I wonder how long she's been without water?' Cassie said, looking at the empty bottle.

'We'll bring some back with us,' said Becky, as the girls started moving away.

'Hurry!' Cassie called, as she began again rubbing Emily's cold hands and talking to her.

Emily didn't speak again but Cassie knew, even in the dark, that for one or two moments at least, her friend was conscious that she was there with her.

The despair and loneliness which Emily must have felt in the dark tunnel pervaded Cassie's senses as she waited for her friends to come back. After what seemed like hours, but was in reality only a few minutes, Cassie saw welcome beams of light coming towards her.

Poppy had brought Miss Eiseldown with her. She knelt beside Emily and whispered words of encouragement to her.

'Do you think she can hear me?' she asked, turning to the two girls.

'I'm sure she is half aware, at least some of the time,' said Cassie.

'Miss Wrench and Matron are making some phone calls,' said Miss Eiseldown. 'The ambulance shouldn't be too long. We mustn't move her ourselves.'

'Can we give her a drink?' asked Cassie.

'I should think so,' said Miss Eiseldown. 'If she comes round enough.'

Cassie managed to get Emily to swallow a couple of mouthfuls, but their housemother cautioned her against giving her any more. In any case, Emily sank into unconsciousness again.

Miss Eiseldown stood and played the torch across the ceiling and walls of the tunnel.

'Fancy your stumbling across this!' she said. 'It was very lucky for Emily you did. But, come to think of it, how did *Emily* find it?'

Cassie thought the time had come to tell all. 'We found it when we were doing the Unders and Overs,' she explained.

'Oh yes, I remember. When Poppy came through Miss Oakland's ceiling. Does the tunnel lead anywhere?'

'Yes,' answered Cassie. 'To the folly, near the wood.'

'Good heavens!' exclaimed Miss Eiseldown. 'It's a wonder it hadn't been blocked up.'

'It had,' Cassie admitted. 'But we made a way through.'

Miss Eiseldown was silent with astonishment.

'I suppose Emily thought of it as a pretty secret place to hide. Poor thing. It must have been terrible for her, down here, on her own,' she said, after a while.

In a surprisingly short time, the ambulance men arrived, led by Becky, and carrying a stretcher. As Emily was being lifted carefully on to it, she opened her eyes again.

'Am I home?' she whispered.

'Not yet,' said Miss Eiseldown. 'But soon, very soon.'

'Don't worry, Em,' said Cassie, stroking her hair away from her clammy forehead. 'Everything's going to be all right.'

The little procession made its way back along the tunnel and through the cellar rooms, with Becky as its guide, and Cassie and Poppy bringing up the rear.

As the stretcher emerged into the daylight of the corridor, Cassie saw that Matron and Miss Wrench were both waiting there. Miss Wrench stepped forward and a look of horror passed over her features when she saw the state that Emily was in.

'I've phoned your mother,' she said gently to the unconscious girl. 'If you can hear me, Emily, you're no longer suspended. I'll make sure you have a place in the third year. Just get better, that's all.'

She looked round at Matron, at a loss for anything else to say.

'I don't think she can hear you, Miss Wrench,' said Matron.

But Cassie thought she had. When she looked closely at Emily's mouth, she thought she saw the glimmer of a smile.

Emily was quickly whisked away to the ambulance which drove away with its siren wailing dramatically.

Once the girls were alone again, Cassie rushed back to her room to get some money.

'What's that for?' asked Becky, as Cassie rushed past her on her way out of the room.

'For the pay-phone,' said Cassie.

'Oh, of course, yes!' cried Becky. 'We've got to phone Emily's dad.'

Mr Pickering was overjoyed when Cassie told him Emily had been found. She told him which hospital she had been taken to, but he didn't say whether or not he would visit her.

'I doubt if he will,' said Becky, after the phonecall.

'He's very secretive,' said Poppy. 'He'll probably just phone the hospital anonymously to see if she's all right.'

'I know what I must do,' said Becky. 'Go and see how Hammy is at Abigail's. I didn't have the chance for a proper look at him earlier.'

Cassie and Poppy went with her, as they didn't feel at all in the mood for doing their homework. When they entered the room, Abi was playing with Hammy on the floor, while Celia sat sulking in the corner.

'I've sworn Celia to secrecy,' said Abigail.

Cassie wondered privately how Abi had managed that, but guessed by the look on Celia's face, that Abi must have used some awful threat.

'How's Hammy settling in?' Becky asked.

'Fine,' said Abigail. 'No problem at all. How did Emily seem before they got her in the ambulance?'

'It's difficult to tell,' said Cassie. 'She looked very ill, very thin and frail somehow.'

'They'll know how to look after her properly in hospital,' said Becky.

'And Miss Wrench has lifted her suspension,' said Cassie. 'I'm sure Emily heard her say that.'

'Oh that's great,' said Abi. 'Let's hope she gets better quickly.'

First thing the next morning, Miss Eiseldown found a small delegation of girls at her door. Cassie, Becky and Poppy had come to plead with her to take them to see Emily in hospital.

'I've no idea if they'll let us see her yet,' said their housemother. 'It is rather early days.'

'Oh please, Miss Eiseldown,' said Cassie. 'Couldn't you phone up and see if we could visit?'

'Well, all right,' Miss Eiseldown sighed, admitting

defeat. 'I'll let you know later. But don't raise your hopes.'

Just after break, Miss Eiseldown got a message to the girls to meet her in her room at the beginning of their lunch-hour.

'The hospital must have said yes!' said Cassie.

When they found Miss Eiseldown at one o'clock, she already had her jacket on.

'Come on,' she said. 'We won't have much time. And I'm afraid it means skipping lunch.'

Poppy and Cassie both looked at Becky. She shrugged.

'I'm getting used to missing meals,' she said.

When they found Emily's ward, the sister in charge explained she was in a room to herself and still needed special care.

'Don't excite her at all,' she warned the girls. 'But I think it will cheer her up to see you. She's had no visitors today.'

'Hasn't her mother been to see her?' asked Miss Eiseldown in surprise.

'Oh yes, she was with her till late last night. But she had to get back to make proper arrangements for her other children. She's coming back later today and staying at the hospital till Emily's discharged. We have facilities, you know, for mothers to stay in the children's ward.'

The girls crept into Emily's room, with their teacher, and were pleased to find her awake, though looking very tired.

'Hello,' she said quietly.

Cassie squeezed her hand. 'You've got to get better in record time,' she said. 'We miss you.'

'And we need you in our team for the tap dancing marathon,' said Becky.

Emily smiled weakly.

'We mean it,' said Poppy.

'I've brought you Little Ted to look after you while you're in here,' said Cassie, offering Emily her little teddy-bear.

'Thanks for everything,' Emily murmured. 'What's all this about tap dancing?'

As the girls launched into their charity stunt idea, Miss Eiseldown interrupted, from the door.

'I can see Emily's mother coming down the corridor,' she said. 'Time to go, I think!'

'Oh,' said Cassie, in a disappointed tone. 'We've only just got here.'

'I'm sorry,' said Miss Eiseldown firmly, 'but Emily mustn't get over-excited, remember?'

The friends reluctantly said their goodbyes, promising to come back if they could, and left the room just as Mrs Pickering reached the door.

Her hard feelings against the school must have softened, because she shook Miss Eiseldown's hand and greeted her politely.

Then she turned to the girls.

'I don't know how to thank you,' she said. 'If you hadn't found Emily when you did, I don't like to think what would have happened.'

She brushed away a tear with the back of her hand.

'The doctors told me she would only have lasted

133

another few hours without water or food. She was on the verge of a coma when you got to her.'

Cassie found it hard to know what to say, but Becky managed a reply: 'She's going to be fine now. It'll be great to have her back!'

Cassie knew what Becky meant by that last sentence. It would be great to have the old Emily back. But how could anyone be sure they would?

As the girls trooped down the long corridor, followed by their teacher, Cassie saw a man coming towards them with a large bunch of red roses.

'Oh no,' she hissed to Becky. 'Sister can't have told him that Emily's mother is there.'

'Do you think we should tell him?' whispered Becky.

By then, Mr Pickering had reached them. He looked haggard and tired.

'How does Emily seem?' he asked them anxiously.

'Quite chirpy,' said Miss Eiseldown, 'and she's in the best place, isn't she?'

'Oh yes,' he said. 'I'll just go along and see her, then.'

Despite his words, he remained rooted to the spot. Cassie saw how much effort it had cost him to get this far. If they mentioned Mrs Pickering being here now, he'd probably never have the courage to come back.

She started walking, tacitly encouraging the others to join her, and allowing him to continue his own journey. When Cassie dared to look back a few moments later, he had disappeared into Emily's room. Cassie lingered for a little while, watching. He didn't come out.

* * *

When they got back to school, there was quite a different sort of meeting on their landing. As the girls and Miss Eiseldown made their way down it, they were confronted by a speeding golden hamster, being chased by two shrieking girls. These turned out to be Abigail and Celia.

Hammy shot through Miss Eiseldown's legs, leaving her gasping with astonishment.

Cassie's mind felt so much lighter and clearer, now she had seen Emily. Her reactions must have sharpened up too, for, almost without knowing what she was doing, she flung herself after the hamster and grabbed him.

'You'd better give him to me quickly,' said Becky, 'in case he affects you.'

Miss Eiseldown had turned to the girls, hands on hips. 'And who does this animal belong to?' she asked.

There was a silence. Celia opened her mouth, but Abigail glared at her so fiercely that she shut it again without a word.

'I see,' said Miss Eiseldown, taking in the situation. 'Then, Rebecca, I consign this waif and stray to your tender loving care, until something can be fixed up.'

'I could take him home with me at Easter,' said Becky eagerly. 'I've got loads of pets. One more wouldn't make any difference.'

'No,' said Miss Eiseldown, smiling wryly. 'I don't suppose it would.'

135

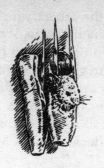

12

Better News

With Hammy installed in his cage in the bathroom and Emily comfortable in hospital, the girls felt happier than they had done for some time. Permission had been granted for their charity event and so they were spending every spare moment when they weren't rehearsing *Cinderella* organising the tap dancing marathon.

In the end, they had enough volunteers from throughout the school to form ten small groups. Mr Whistler was very helpful and made sure all those taking part were excused from lessons the following Saturday, which was to be the big day. Permission also had to be sought from their housemothers to dance the night away.

This had been the aspect which Mr Whistler had most trouble persuading Miss Wrench about, but in the end he had won her round by emphasising the sacrifice involved in giving up a night's sleep.

With just a few days to go, all the preparations had been made. All but one, that is. Cassie still had an important phonecall to make. Instead of the school pay-phone, Cassie decided to ask Mrs Allingham if she could use hers.

That lunch-time, she and Becky ran across to her cottage, in a downpour which soaked them, even through their raincoats.

'Oh my goodness,' the old lady said, when she saw them. 'You'll catch your death, the pair of you. Come in by the fire and I'll fetch some towels.'

As the girls towelled their hair dry, and let their wet garments steam over the fireguard, they told their friend about their plan.

'Sounds a lovely idea,' said Mrs Allingham. 'Can I come and watch? At least, the daytime part of the event.'

'Of course you can,' Cassie agreed. 'In fact, you can be the adjudicator to check no one's cheating. Mr Whistler said he might not be able to in the day because of his classes.'

'That's settled then,' said Mrs Allingham, beaming. 'Now, Cassie, you said you wanted to use the phone?'

'Yes please. I've got the money here for the call.'

Cassie dialled the number carefully and took a deep breath. She had never telephoned a newspaper office before.

'Hello. Newsdesk.'

'Hi. This is Cassandra Brown from Redwood Ballet School.'

'Hold on. That's the place that the student ran away from, isn't it? I'll put you through to Joe. He dealt with the story.'

Cassie was put through to Joe, and introduced herself to him.

'Have you got a tip-off for us, kid?' he asked.

'Yes,' said Cassie. 'We're going to hold a charity stunt on Saturday and we're hoping you'll send a reporter round.'

'Oh, er, that sounds nice, but it's not quite our thing, I'm afraid,' said Joe, rather less enthusiastically.

'It's funny isn't it,' said Cassie, 'how the bad things always get reported and the good ones hardly ever do?'

'Now that's not true, you know,' said Joe.

'I think you owe it to us,' said Cassie, more fiercely than she'd intended. 'You gave the school a bad name when you wrote that article about my friend running away and, when she'd been found, you only put in a few lines about it.'

'Well, there wasn't much to say, was there,' said Joe rather sheepishly, 'only that she'd been taken to hospital.'

'You could have said that we'd found her, not the police,' said Cassie hotly, 'and that she'd been hiding in an underground tunnel for days and only we knew the secret of its whereabouts. And you could have said Miss Wrench had lifted her suspension and —'

'Hang on a minute,' said Joe. 'I'm trying to take this down. We didn't know about any of this. It's great stuff!'

'Now,' said Cassie, 'you are going to send a reporter to our tap dancing marathon on Saturday, aren't you? I'll tell you more then. We're starting at nine in the morning and dancing right through the night!'

'I'll come myself!' said Joe.

'Promise?'

'Promise.'

Cassie had one more hurdle to leap before Saturday; she had to keep the long-awaited appointment with the chest specialist in the Queen Elizabeth hospital.

Her mother picked her up on Friday morning just as the bell sounded for morning break.

'Good luck!' called Becky and Poppy, as she left with Joy.

A short drive took them to the carpark of the hospital. Cassie had been unable to get in again to see Emily, and so she seized this opportunity to ask her mum if they could visit her after their appointment.

Joy was a bit reluctant. 'I know you want to see her, darling, but it really depends on how long it takes us.'

'Oh, please Mum, I hardly got a chance to speak to her at all when Miss Eiseldown brought us in.'

'Well, we'll see,' said Joy.

When they were kept waiting for over an hour, Cassie was glad that her mum had been thoughtful enough to bring a book for her to read. At last, her name was called and a nurse led them into a small consulting room, where Mr Perkins, the specialist, sat at his desk. He was white-haired and bespectacled.

'Well, young lady, have you been experiencing any more wheezing since your doctor wrote to me?'

'Yes and no,' said Cassie.

Mr Perkins peered at her over the top of his straight-edged glasses.

'I mean, I've had a few attacks,' said Cassie, 'but none recently.'

'Ah, I see.' The doctor consulted her notes. 'It may be that the brown inhaler is beginning to work then.'

'No, I don't think it's that,' said Cassie excitedly. Joy gave her a nudge, as Mr Perkins again looked at her over the top of his spectacles.

'What do you think it is, then, young lady?' he asked.

'Well, my friend Becky, who wants to be a vet, looked my symptoms up in a book and . . . she was the one who diagnosed my asthma first, by the way!'

'*Was* she indeed?' exclaimed the doctor, raising his eyebrows.

'Yes,' went on Cassie, undeterred by another nudge from her mother, 'and she hit on the cause for my asthma; an allergy to—'

Cassie stopped in mid-flight, suddenly and uncomfortably aware that she might get Becky into trouble if she revealed that she had kept her pet hamster at school.

'An allergy to what?' prompted Mr Perkins, looking more puzzled by the minute.

141

Joy Brown stared at her daughter, who was thinking hard.

'To . . . to hamsters. There was one running round the school and she thought it might have been that,' she finished lamely.

Cassie could see Mr Perkins was trying very hard not to smile. 'Well, you may be allergic to *something*, that's true. We can run some tests to make quite sure. What do you think, Mrs Brown?'

'Oh yes, anything,' replied Joy.

'Let me just listen to your chest, and then you can have a blow into the peak-flow tube.'

After Cassie had been examined, the doctor put down his stethoscope.

'Well, that's very encouraging, I'm pleased to say. It seems as though you're responding very well to your inhalers.'

'Will I be able to continue my dance training?' Cassie blurted out. It was the most important question, as far as she was concerned.

'No reason why not,' he replied. 'Several top athletes have the condition. But of course, the final decision rests with your ballet school.'

Cassie felt relieved by his words, and hardly felt a thing when the nurse injected her with several potential allergens a few minutes later.

'It's not like a full injection,' the nurse explained. 'We're popping the substances just under the skin. And if it comes up in an itchy weal, you'll know you're allergic to it.'

'What sort of substances?' asked Joy.

'Oh, pollen, house-dust, feathers, mould, that sort of thing.'

'Have you got hamster?' asked Cassie.

'Hamster? No, I don't think so,' she laughed. 'But we have got dog and cat hair. Oh, we've got rodent hair – that should do! Do you want me to try that?'

'Yes please,' said Cassie.

After a few minutes, the results were quite plain to see. By the lumps on her arm, Cassie now knew that she was allergic to house-dust, feathers and all the animal hair.

'That means no pets indoors, I'm afraid,' said the nurse to Mrs Brown. 'And make sure none of her bedding or pillows are filled with feathers.'

'What about house-dust?' asked Joy Brown anxiously.

'She's not had a huge reaction, so just keep the dust down with a damp cloth, and hoover regularly.'

'I should think it's pretty clean at school,' said Joy. 'Their rooms are inspected daily.'

'Good,' said the nurse, 'and there won't be any pets there either, will there?'

Cassie rushed into Emily's room, eager to tell her all that had been happening.

'I'll leave you two to chat,' said Joy. 'I'll just pop along to the cafe for a cup of tea.'

'Oh, I'm glad you've come to see me,' said Emily. 'I'm getting bored. Mum's had to go home today – she couldn't leave the little ones any longer.'

'What about your dad?' Cassie asked, wondering if she should mention him.

Emily's face brightened.

'Yes. He comes every night after work.'

Cassie looked carefully at her. Emily's face was rounding out again – she had lost those awful hollow cheeks and dark rings round her eyes. And her eyes looked sparklingly clear.

'Is it all right then now?' asked Cassie. 'I mean with your dad and mum?'

'Dad's coming back home at weekends and as soon as they can sell our house, Mum and the others are moving up here with him.'

'Oh, that's fantastic!' cried Cassie. 'They'll be really close to you at school.'

'It just feels so good that they've made it up,' said Emily. 'If only Dad hadn't stayed away so long! He said he was dying to come back to us all along.'

'Why didn't he, then?'

'He was too ashamed that he'd just walked out like that without a word. It was when he'd lost his job, do you remember my telling you? He was very, very depressed. And once he'd gone, he didn't know how to come back.'

'So he made a new life in Birmingham, did he?' asked Cassie.

'Yes, he got a good job again, too. But he says he missed us all like crazy. And when he went to see *Swan Lake* that night, he just couldn't believe it when he saw me dancing as a little swan.'

'Then came the red roses,' said Cassie.

Emily grinned and pointed to the vases at the opposite end of the room, which were overflowing with crimson blooms. 'He keeps sending me them, even now.'

'Oh, Em, I'm so pleased for you,' cried Cassie, giving her friend a big hug. 'And you look so much better now.'

'I'm eating really well,' Emily said, giggling. 'Like a horse, in fact. Making up for lost time, I suppose.'

'When are you coming back to school?' asked Cassie.

'Sometime next term. The doctors haven't given me a precise date. I've got to get up to a weight target.'

'No tour then?'

'No tour,' said Emily with a touch of regret in her voice.

'Never mind,' said Cassie. 'I'll send you lots of postcards.'

'Are they going to let you go, then?'

'Cross your fingers,' said Cassie. 'I don't know yet, till I've seen the Wrench.'

'Miss Wrench came in to see me with Miss Eiseldown yesterday.'

'Did she? What did she say?'

'She was really nice. She still feels guilty, I think. She knew I would be disappointed about the tour, so we're going to do a special performamce of *Cinderella* next term, for the parents. And I'm going to dance Cinders.'

'That's lovely, Em. I can't wait for you to come back to school. It really doesn't feel right without you there.'

'I'm looking forward to it now. I'm putting all the bad memories behind me.'

Cassie looked at Emily. She wanted to ask her something, but didn't quite know how.

'Emily,' she began.

'Yes?'

'When you come back, you won't . . . you won't start dieting again, will you?'

'No,' said Emily quietly. 'I won't. I know my family's OK now and I know I'm OK. Don't worry, Cassie. I'm cured. I really am!'

After a quick snack in the hospital cafe, Cassie and her mother drove back to school.

'We're going to be a few minutes late for afternoon school, I'm afraid,' said Joy, when they were held up at some roadworks.

Cassie ran through her timetable mentally. Luckily it was Miss Eiseldown taking them for first period, so she wouldn't have a lot of explaining to do.

'Goodbye darling,' said her mum, as she dropped her off in the drive. 'I'll be seeing you again next week. Don't forget our appointment with Miss Wrench!'

'No I won't forget. Bye Mum.'

'Oh, and have fun doing your charity stunt!'

Cassie hoped that Miss Wrench wouldn't start thinking they were having fun. If she did, she might cancel the whole thing.

But when the next day came, there was no hint of cancelled plans. Mr Whistler met the girls in Studio One, straight after breakfast. Cassie, Poppy, Becky and Abigail were the first to arrive, but the room quickly filled up with the other tappers. Other volunteers were manning a snack bar – another money-raising idea – in the small room adjoining the studio. Cassie and her friends had scrounged a pile of magazines which they left at the non-working end of the studio, with a few stacks of chairs, so that kids who weren't actually dancing would have something to do other than eat and drink.

Girls outnumbered boys by about ten to one, but Cassie was pleased to see that Matthew, Tom and Ojo had all volunteered. In fact they were in the first team of dancers, and were putting their tap shoes on, in readiness.

Cassie went over to them.

'Thanks for supporting us,' she said.

'I have my reasons for being here,' said Matthew mysteriously.

'Oh? And what are they?' asked Cassie.

'Well, let's say it's earning me some Brownie points.'

'Who with?'

'My mum. I'm gradually getting round her about the tour. This charity stunt is helping a lot.'

'Oh, that's great,' said Cassie. 'So will you definitely be coming to France?'

'Cross your fingers. I'm nearly there, I think.'

Mr Whistler came across to join the group. 'Cassandra, I have to go off to teach now. What time is Mrs Allingham arriving?'

'I'm expecting her any moment, Mr Whistler. I'll get the first team in position.'

As soon as Mr Whistler left the room, the noise level increased dramatically and Cassie felt glad when Mrs

Allingham bustled in and the proceedings could get under way.

Just as the first team finished their stint, Joe, the newspaper man arrived, notebook in hand, and accompanied by a photographer. All the children present were squashed together at one end of the studio and asked to start tap dancing. Several photographs were taken and then Joe asked Cassie a lot of questions about finding Emily. She answered them freely, but also made sure he was fed plenty of information about their charity event.

The girls kept Mrs Allingham plied with snacks and chatter all day, so that, when twilight approached, she seemed quite reluctant to leave. But Mr Whistler came back then, so she had no excuse to stay any longer.

'Well, thank you so much for inviting me,' she said. 'I haven't had so much fun for ages. And it was lovely watching you all tapping away.'

As the night wore on, the chatting became more subdued, but, under Mr Whistler's scrutiny, the enthusiasm of the dancers never waned. Cassie found the early hours of the morning were the worst; her body was crying out for sleep. Her group danced for the last time at about four in the morning. They were glad of the exercise to wake them up and ease their stiffening joints. After it, they didn't want to feel dozy again, so they swapped places with some of the snack bar helpers, who were eager to get to bed.

'It's the first time I've ever been awake all night,' said Cassie.

'Me too,' said Becky. 'It feels really funny to be awake at this time, doesn't it?'

'Perhaps we should do it more often?'

'Oh no,' groaned Poppy. 'Once is enough!'

Through sponsorship and snackbar sales, the students managed to raise over £500, which they shared between the RSPCA and research into anorexia.

The following Monday morning, Cassie's mother was back again.

'My car's beginning to know its own way to Redwood,' she remarked to her daughter, as they made their way across the hall to Miss Wrench's study.

Miss Wrench listened attentively to Joy's account of what the specialist had said and then sat back in her chair.

'Well, that seems quite satisfactory, Mrs Brown,' she said. 'There's nothing to prevent Cassandra from pursuing her chosen training.'

'Cassandra would very much like to go on the tour and she *does* seem so much better now,' said Joy.

'I don't see why not,' Miss Wrench agreed. 'She'll have to ensure she has her inhalers with her, of course.'

Cassie smiled her relief at her mother.

'While she's here at school, the doctor will monitor her condition very carefully,' went on Miss Wrench, 'so I don't think you need to have any anxiety about her being away from home.'

'Oh, that's reassuring,' said Joy.

Miss Wrench smiled – a very rare occurrence.

'Perhaps I should tell you – in confidence of course – that Cassandra passed her Easter assessment and we'll be pleased to offer her a place for the third year.'

'Oh thank you!' Cassie burst out. She couldn't contain her happiness.

Miss Wrench turned to her. 'You'll just have to be more dedicated and more careful than the average student. And try to channel all your surplus energy into practising your dancing.'

As the Principal's eyes bored into hers, Cassie blushed.

'Now, I expect you want to tell your mother all about the tap dancing event you helped to organise.'

'She already has!' said Joy, laughing. 'There's not much of ballet school life that I don't get to hear about.'

Miss Wrench pulled out a newspaper from one of her desk drawers.

'Have you seen this?' she asked.

A photograph of the tap dancers, with Cassie and her friends in the front row, was above the caption:

REDWOOD STUDENT RECOVERS AS FRIENDS HELP CHARITY IN ALL NIGHT TAP MARATHON

Though not on the front page this time, the article about Redwood which followed was quite detailed and prominent. And even more important, complimentary.

No wonder the Wrench is being nice to me, thought Cassie.

'It makes a change to see young people getting a good press,' said her mother.

'Well, I admire these youngsters for putting some effort into raising money for charity,' said Miss Wrench, getting up. 'Thank you, Mrs Brown, for coming in. I'm sure with support at home and at school, Cassandra will be fine. She is a promising student and we should have been sorry to lose her!'

Cassie tripped out of the study, with her feet on air, and dashed off to tell her friends she would be joining them on tour.

'Even if I *am* only in the corps de ballet, I don't care. At least I'm going!' she yelled to her room-mates, as she bounced up and down on her bed.

'Won't Madame give you back your solo?' asked Poppy.

'No, I doubt it,' said Cassie, sitting down with a bump. 'It wouldn't be fair on Celia now, would it?'

'I suppose not.'

When they got to the *Cinderella* rehearsal that evening, Madame asked them all to sit down on the floor for a moment.

'As some of you know, *mes eleves*,' she began, 'Emily will not be able to come on tour in France with us this time.'

There were murmurs of commiseration in the studio.

'And so we must choose a new understudy for

Cinderella and fill the part of the Spring Fairy also. Miss Oakland and I are pleased to offer both parts to Cassandra Brown.'

Cassie stared at her ballet mistress for a moment, before breaking into a delighted grin.

'And Celia will keep Cassandra's old solo.'

It was Celia's turn to look as pleased as Punch.

As the rehearsal got under way, Cassie realised that a very big task lay ahead of her. Not only had she the Spring solo to learn, which involved some very fast and intricate footwork, but she also had to shadow Abigail throughout her appearances in the ballet.

She was less daunted when Madame explained that as she was coming to the part so late, they would not be expecting her to dance Cinderella in any of the performances abroad, except in the unlikely event of Abigail's falling ill.

Thus, Cassie put her fullest attention over the last few weeks of term into learning the Spring solo.

'You've picked up Emily's dance ever so quickly,' Poppy said to her in the changing-rooms, after their penultimate rehearsal.

'Yes, it's fantastic,' said Becky. 'And you've had to learn Abi's part as well!'

'Well, I'm not confident of all of that,' Cassie confessed.

'Can you believe we'll be in France this time next week?' Becky exclaimed.

'And to think I might not have been coming at all,' said Cassie. 'I just wish Emily was too.'

'Matthew reckons he's definitely coming,' said Becky.

'Yes,' said Poppy, 'but he's had to promise his mum he'll do homework for six hours a day when he's home next week.'

'Good job it's only three days,' laughed Becky. 'It is a pity though, about Emily.'

'Shame it couldn't be Celia staying behind instead really,' said Poppy wistfully.

Celia popped up just at that moment with Abigail, but fortunately, she didn't show any sign of overhearing the last remark.

'Hi you guys,' she said. 'Can't wait for next week to come round, can you?'

She linked arms with Abigail who gave an apologetic smile before sauntering off with Celia in tow.

'Perhaps Celia will be better company than we'd thought!' said Poppy.

'I reckon Abi must have promised to be best friends with her, in turn for keeping Hammy a secret,' said Becky thoughtfully.

'Will you miss Hammy very much?' Cassie asked her friend.

'No, it'll be a relief really to take him home tomorrow,' said Becky with a giggle. 'And I'll still be able to see Tinker whenever I want at Mrs Allingham's.'

Cassie smiled. She could foresee nothing to cast a blemish on either the Easter tour or the following term.

And beyond that . . . the future stretched out before her like a vast unpainted canvas. Would a figure be etched upon it – a little ballerina with Cassie's face? More than anything in the world, she hoped it would be so. But she knew that only time would tell.